MARCIA LYNN McCLURE

Published by Distractions Ink
1290 Mirador Loop N.E.
Rio Rancho, NM 87144

Published by Distractions Ink

Cover Photography by ©Nyul/Dreamstime.com
and ©Irina Ukrainets/Dreamstime.com
Cover Design and Interior Graphics by Sandy Ann Allred/Timeless Allure

First Printed Edition: March 2015

All character names and personalities in this work of fiction are entirely fictional, created solely in the imagination of the author.
Any resemblance to any person living or dead is coincidental.

McClure, Marcia Lynn, 1965—
With a Dreamboat in a Hammock: a novel/by Marcia Lynn McClure.

ISBN: 978-0-9861307-3-1

Printed in the United States of America

To my beautiful, cherished
and infinitely loved daughter, Sandy:

Mere words can never express my love and admiration
for the wonderful, talented woman you are—
for the loving, fun, caring, and kind wife and mother you are.
Still, for the sake that we share such a deep
reverence and appreciation
for history, photos, and photography,
I dedicate this book to you—
Because of our shared love for the
miraculous beauty of photography!

CHAPTER ONE

Valynn tried to sit still—tried not to fidget—but her nerves were getting the best of her. She wanted the restorer's position at Wolfe Photography so badly she could taste it!

She considered it a miracle that she'd even managed to land an interview. Yet, as afraid as she was to get her hopes up, they were up—way up! Valynn knew that if she could manage to secure the position at Wolfe Photography, then she really *could* make a good living using her photographic skills—and that was something she'd wanted ever since she'd been a little girl.

Smoothing the skirt of her brown business suit, Valynn reached down to the side of her chair to make sure her portfolio was still there. She knew it would be but was nevertheless relieved to know that it hadn't somehow grown legs and walked away. It was her only hope of getting the job—the proof that she really was as good at photo restoration as she'd claimed to be on her application. For one thing, Valynn knew that the moment the interviewer—a woman named Paula Jackson—saw her, she would make the assumption (just as everyone else always did) that Valynn was far too young to be even a mediocre restorer, let alone a superior one. After all, it would be a natural assumption for anyone—that Valynn couldn't possibly be as accomplished as she was—not when she was only twenty years old, especially when she didn't look a day over eighteen. But she *was* accomplished, and her portfolio was the proof of it.

The door to a room adjoining the reception area opened. A tall, slender, very pretty, middle-aged woman appeared, smiled at Valynn, and asked, "Valynn Wickley?"

"That's me!" Valynn exclaimed, hopping to her feet. Adrenaline was pumping through her body like water through a Super Soaker.

The woman smiled, offering a hand to Valynn. "I'm Paula Jackson. It's nice to meet you."

Valynn smiled and accepted the woman's handshake in greeting. "It's nice to meet you, Ms. Jackson."

Paula Jackson's smile broadened, and she laughed a little. "Oh, just call me Paula. We're not that formal around here."

"Okay," Valynn agreed—though she thought that the woman's incredibly classy business slacks and blouse looked far from casual. She was glad she'd worn her own business skirt and jacket.

"Let's head on into my office and talk a bit, all right?" Paula asked, stepping aside and gesturing that Valynn should precede her.

"Of course," Valynn agreed. She could feel her hands shaking as she reached down, taking hold of the handle of her portfolio case before striding into the room Paula Jackson indicated.

"I was very impressed with the samples you e-mailed to us, Valynn," Paula began. "None of the other applicants' work looked as good as yours."

Again, Valynn tried not to let her hopes leap too high inside her—but again it was too late. "Thank you," she breathed with relief. "I love restoring, and maybe that's the difference, right? To me, it's more than just a job. It's a necessity, you know? Photography is changing so much, and I'm not sure the average Joe realizes the importance of protecting and digitally cataloging old photographs."

Paula smiled, nodded, and said, "I agree. And thankfully, our clients don't seem to fall into that average Joe category. In fact, we're getting more and more clients asking for restoration of old family photos. And of course, Mr. Wolfe has his own vast collection of vintage photos and negatives."

"Oh yes!" Valynn nearly squealed with excitement. "It was his site—the one where he posts scans of his favorites—that's how I first became aware that you all were looking for someone to work on restoration for you."

Paula smiled, motioning that Valynn should take a seat in a chair facing a desk. "Well, that restoration you did on the old school class portrait was phenomenal! Mr. Wolfe was very impressed."

Valynn bit her lip with barely restrained delight. "Oh, I'm so glad!" she almost giggled. "Wolfe Photography has such an incredible reputation. I can't believe I'm even here for an interview!"

Paula laughed a little, took her own seat in the chair behind her desk, and studied Valynn for a moment.

"You have incredible talent, especially considering how young you are, Miss Wickley," she began.

"Oh, it's Valynn, please," Valynn interjected.

Paula nodded and continued, "And everyone who has seen the examples of your work that you e-mailed to us is awed."

"Thank you," Valynn said.

"And I see you did bring a portfolio with you," Paula asked.

"Yes," Valynn said. Quickly, yet carefully, she opened her portfolio, laying it on the desk before Paula. "There are a few restored portraits, of course. I'm guessing that's what most people come to you for, being that portraits are what I spend ninety percent of my time restoring. But I've also included some landscapes, basic snapshots, and anything else I could think of off the top of my head. I tried to select some of my favorites."

Valynn watched closely as Paula slowly leafed through the copies of restored photographs in the portfolio. The woman seemed pleased—smiled and nodded often, even arched her classy, perfectly plucked eyebrows in admiration multiple times.

"Incredible!" Paula exclaimed at last. She smiled at Valynn, asking, "Do you mind waiting here a moment while I show these to one other person, real quick?"

"Not at all," Valynn answered. She forced a smile and tried to appear calm—though she felt more nervous than even she had a moment before. She thought Paula Jackson was the person who would or would not hire her. She hadn't realized there would be someone else in the hiring mix.

She watched as Paula left the room by way of a side door. Exhaling a heavy sigh, Valynn literally crossed her fingers where her hands lay in her lap and tried to remain hopeful. After all, the portfolio contained before restoration and after restoration copies of each photograph included, and Valynn knew they were examples of her best work. Yet she couldn't help wondering if her best might not be good enough for Wolfe Photography.

Paula smiled as she knocked on the door to Jensen's office. She knew that the young woman sitting in her own office was far and away the best restorer that had applied for the position. Furthermore, she liked the girl—liked her excitement and obvious love of photographs—liked her energy and even the fact that she was so young.

Still, Paula did feel as if she should run the final decision past Jensen one more time—even though he'd given her full rein on whom to hire for the position. And besides, Paula wanted him to see the portfolio Valynn Wickley had brought with her. The examples of her work were phenomenal, and she knew Jensen would enjoy them.

"Come in," Jensen called from the other side of the door. He looked up when Paula entered the room, grinned, and said, "Hey, Paula. What's going on?"

Paula hurried to his desk, laying the open portfolio out before him.

"I just thought I'd show you some of the work done by my number one choice for the restorer's position. You know, just so you agree that this is the best stuff that's crossed your desk," she explained.

Jensen chuckled, shaking his head, even as he began to study the copies of restored photos lying before him.

"I told you that this is your call, Paula," he reminded her. "I trust you implicitly on this, you know."

Paula shrugged. "Yeah, I know. But this work is too incredible not to share with you. Are you just blown away or what?"

She watched as Jensen studied the photos, each one, very carefully. He even picked up one of the many magnifying glasses scattered over his desk to get a better view of some of the details.

"Dang!" he exclaimed under his breath. "You're right. This is incredible work." Jensen sat back in his chair, asking, "How much are we offering to pay this guy?"

"She's a woman. And didn't we decide on twenty-five dollars an hour? Or were you still batting the idea around that a salary per project would be better?" Paula asked.

But Jensen shook his head. "Nope, let's go with the hourly wage. I want to lock this woman in with Wolfe Photography, and an hourly wage is more secure, you know?" he answered.

"But what if we don't have the consistent restoring jobs at first?" Paula inquired. She wanted to give Valynn a solid job—full time or part time—either way, something she could depend on so the talented young woman wouldn't feel like she needed to shop around for a more stable position somewhere else.

"Guarantee her thirty hours a week, and hopefully she'll take that," Jensen said. "She can work on some things I want done for my own stuff if the clients don't roll in fast enough at first," he said. "But let her know we'll get her up to forty hours, if she wants that many, as soon as we can, all right?" He paused a moment, his eyes narrowing as he studied some photographs tucked into a pocket in the back of the portfolio. He turned one over and read aloud what was written on the back. "*Valynn Wickley.*"

Paula watched as Jensen looked through all the photos in the pocket of the portfolio.

"Looks like she has a fantastic eye," he said. "Maybe she'd be willing to help out on shoots if the restoration work takes awhile to build up." Jensen carefully closed the portfolio, leaned back in his chair again, and said, "Ask her if she'd be willing to help out on away shoots and stuff too, and then offer her thirty to forty hours a week at the hourly wage. All right?"

"You bet," Paula said as she gathered up the portfolio. "Um…she's in my office right now, if you'd like to meet her, Jensen."

But as she expected, Jensen frowned and shook his head. "Not today, Paula. I trust your judgment. Just give her the offer, and let's get her to work on the restoration stuff we have waiting as soon as she can start, okay?"

"Roger that, boss," Paula said.

She watched as Jensen returned to his computer and began scrolling through digital images of a recent shoot he'd done of a well-to-do family uptown. For a moment, she wondered if maybe she should tell him that Valynn Wickley was young—very young—and that she was a pretty blue-eyed brunette, with a vivacious personality that might well serve to distract some of the guys in the office here and there—even Jensen.

Paula decided not to mention it to Jensen, however. After all, what did it matter? Valynn's work was a profound testament to her talent and obvious ability to do the job. So why did it matter that she was a beautiful young woman who might turn Jensen's head once in a while? After all, Paula knew that once Valynn got a look at Jensen Wolfe, her head would probably spin right off her neck with wanting a second one.

Jensen was younger than Paula by twenty years, but the tall, black-haired, blue-eyed, square-jawed entrepreneur photographer still turned her own head on occasion. She smiled, thinking she hoped she would be present to witness the first time Valynn got a load of her new boss, the drop-dead gorgeous Jensen Wolfe. She wondered if the girl would blush, gasp, and stand there gawking at him with her mouth hanging open the way most women did the first time they saw him.

"I'll let you know how it turns out," Paula said as she turned to leave.

"I want this woman working for us, Paula," Jensen said. "Give her what she wants—you know, realistically."

"Will do," Paula assured him. Smiling to herself, she whispered, "This oughta be fun to watch."

Valynn straightened her posture as Paula Jackson returned to her office.

"Well," the woman said, handing Valynn's portfolio back to her. Valynn's heart was beating so hard with rising hope and nervous anxiety that she could hardly breathe!

"How does twenty-five dollars an hour to start, thirty to forty hours a week, sound?" Paula asked.

Valynn gasped and held her breath. "T-twenty-five an hour?"

"Yep," Paula answered. "I figured I'd just come in with the top number and see if it sounds good enough to you. But I need to add that we would like for you to assist during shoots and stuff here and there if the restoration business takes a while to gain enough momentum to employ you for forty hours of restoration work a week. Does that sound all right?"

"Does that sound all right?" Valynn squealed with delight, leaping to her feet. "That sounds awesome, Ms. Jackson!"

"Paula," Paula corrected as she giggled a bit, obviously amused by Valynn's reaction to the job offer.

Valynn watched as Paula opened a desk drawer and withdrew a small stack of papers secured with a paperclip.

Offering them to Valynn, she said, "Here's the W-2 info and employee reference sheet I'll need you to bring with you when you start." She paused, frowned a little, and asked, "When *can* you start?"

Valynn accepted the paperwork and answered, "The minute you want me to!"

Paula sighed, seeming relieved. "Tomorrow morning? Eight a.m.?"

"Absolutely!" Valynn exclaimed with a giggle of instant joy. "I'm so excited! And so grateful for the opportunity, Paula. You won't regret hiring me. I promise."

Paula smiled. "Oh, I know," she said. "I'll get the employment and salary agreement printed out for you to sign tomorrow, and we'll just get you busy, okay?"

"Of course!" Valynn assured her. She offered her hand to Paula. When Paula accepted her offer of a handshake, Valynn added, "Thank you, Paula. Truly. You have no idea how excited I am to be doing *anything* with Wolfe Photography…especially restoration work. Thank you so much."

"You're welcome, Valynn," Paula said. Her smile broadened, and she said, "Your work is incredible, and we're going to have some very satisfied restoration customers. I can already tell you that."

"I sure hope so," Valynn sighed. The excitement that was welling inside her chest was causing her to feel almost breathless! She felt like she needed to run out of the building, spin around on the front steps, and literally squeal with joy. Instead, she tried to fake the appearance of self-control.

Paula shrugged then, adding, "Well, I guess we'll see you first thing in the morning. Just meet me here in my office, and I'll give you the tour and show you the room we've got set up with everything you'll need…hopefully everything you'll need to start anyway."

"Okay, great!" Valynn said. "I'll be back tomorrow."

"Have a nice afternoon, Valynn," Paula said as Valynn gathered her portfolio.

"You too, Paula," Valynn said.

Then, turning and walking from Paula Jackson's office, Valynn managed to maintain the appearance of calm—until she had exited the building, that is.

Once outside the building that housed the Wolfe Photography office, however, she whirled around, squealing with delight.

She'd landed it! She'd actually landed a job with Wolfe Photography!

Reaching into her purse, Valynn removed her victory Snickers bar. Tearing into it like a hungry lion, she took a bite and began to chew.

"Mmm!" she moaned as the sweet taste of chocolate, caramel, peanuts, and success mingled in her mouth. "I did it," she mumbled. "I actually did it."

She started for the parking lot then, walking her classiest I-know-how-to-walk-in-high-heels walk, and not caring a whit if her hips swung a bit too exaggeratedly. She deserved to enjoy a moment of confidence. It would be a fleeting moment, she knew, so why not savor it for the short time it did last?

After all, she, Valynn Bree Wickley, was now an employee of Wolfe Photography—the best and most respected photography business in the city.

"Mmm," Valynn moaned as she took another bite of her victory Snickers. "Success tastes so good!"

CHAPTER TWO

As always, Jensen felt physically worn out but stoked after his workout. If it hadn't been for the fact that he had to meet Rozlyn for dinner, he'd call it a perfect day and hit the sack early. However, if he didn't meet Rozlyn for dinner, she'd give him a tongue-lashing, and he'd feel like a sack that had been hit.

Jensen exhaled a heavy sigh as he unlocked the back door to the building that housed the offices of Wolfe Photography. He'd left a flash drive on his desk that he'd wanted to take home with him, and if he hurried, he could still get home, showered, and ready to meet Rozlyn at eight at Le Porte Rouge for dinner.

He rushed into his office and started rummaging through the junk on his desk in search of the flash drive. Jensen paused for a moment, however, raked his fingers through his hair, and mumbled, "Why am I even dating Roz?"

It was a question he'd asked himself over and over again—especially during the past week. Sure, Rozlyn Dawson was beautiful—tall, with jet-black hair and dark brown eyes. He'd met her while doing a shoot for a fashion magazine layout, after all. But beyond that, she was kind of a piece of work—bossy, conceited, and always expecting to be wined and dined. The truth was, Jensen was pretty sure he was just a trophy guy to Roz—a young entrepreneur taller than her supermodel height who she could brag about to her friends.

"This is Jensen," Roz would always begin when introducing Jensen to someone. "Isn't he gorgeous? And he's so successful! He owns the most popular, thriving photography studio in town!" It was embarrassing—a downright humiliating way to be introduced.

It always began the same way: he was gorgeous and made a lot of money. It was all Roz ever pointed out about him. Still, the woman had never criticized his appearance—never pointed out the physical characteristic he was most self-conscious about and had been since he was a kid. Was that why he put up with her? Jensen wondered. Or was he as pathetically lonely as he sometimes felt? Did he date Roz simply for something to do? Someone to talk to, even though she rarely listened to anything he had to say?

It certainly wasn't the physicality of their relationship that found Jensen continuing to put up with Rozlyn's…Rozlyn's…well, basically Rozlyn. They'd done their share of kissing, and Roz was always pressuring Jensen to sleep with her—getting furious when he wouldn't. And no matter how many times he tried to explain to her that he wasn't a man-slut—that he didn't believe in sleeping around or casual sex, that he was of the opinion that sex should wait for marriage—she continued to push him.

So why? Jensen thought, frowning. Why did he continue to date her?

Exhaling a heavy sigh, Jensen shoved the USB drive into the pocket of his black mesh workout shorts and turned to leave. Yet as he stepped out of his office and into the hallway, he heard music coming from the right of the corridor. Glancing down the hallway, he saw light flooding from one of the smaller offices.

"Who's working this late?" he mumbled as he strode toward the room where the light and music beamed out into the hallway.

What Jensen Wolfe saw when he reached the threshold of the room caused his eyebrows to arch up in astonishment. In front of a computer with her back to the door stood a young woman. Her long brown hair was pulled up in a ponytail, which swished and swayed back and forth as she danced to the music playing through the computer's speakers.

Jensen couldn't keep from grinning as he watched the young woman lean over the computer keyboard and type in a long succession of keystrokes—as she began singing along to Bruno Mars, "Uptown Funk."

He suppressed a chuckle of amusement as, after singing a few more lines of the song, the young woman dressed in jeans, running shoes, and a simple pink shirt continued to dance as she sang—dance very well and pretty darn provocatively.

Intrigued beyond anything he'd experienced in a long time, Jensen folded his arms across his chest, leaned against the door frame, and simply continued to watch the young woman. He was curious as to how long it would take her to sense she was no longer alone. For a moment, he wondered who the girl was. But in the next instant, he remembered that Paula had indeed hired a woman to work for the company restoring photos. Paula hadn't mentioned, however, that the woman she hired was so young—or that she could sing and dance like she'd stepped directly out of a music video.

Again the girl made a couple of keystroke moves on the keyboard. The high-end printer next to the computer she was working on heated up and began to print. In a few seconds, the printer spat out an image, and the energetic girl snapped the page up and held it out at arm's length to study it.

"There you are, you beautiful thing!" she exclaimed. "Gorgeous, gorgeous, gorgeous! *Ay caramba*!"

The girl paused in studying the printed image to dance a bit. Then, as the song wound to a repeat of the chorus, the girl spun around, smiling and obviously so caught up in the song that it took her a few moments to look up and realize she was no longer alone.

Jensen almost laughed out loud when the girl looked up at him—her very blue, very brilliant, and bright eyes widening as she mumbled, "Yikes!"

"Hi," he said, attempting to look as cool and calm as he could. He was the boss, after all, and he had found a brand-new employee working in the computer room after hours. It stood to reason he should appear as intimidating as possible—at least until he found out why she was there.

"Hi," the young woman said in return. She blushed, and the pink rising to her cheeks only enhanced her attractiveness. Still, Jensen stood firm, arms still folded across his chest as he reminded himself he was the boss—Jensen Wolfe, owner of Wolfe Photography.

"Did you need to lock up?" the girl asked. "I'm so sorry if you were waiting on me. Paula said I could finish up this project before I left today. I didn't want to leave this beautiful vintage woman with a crack still across her face overnight, you know?" she said, holding up the printed copy of a truly lovely Edwardian bride. "I mean, she'd been cracked for so long," the girl continued. "I just couldn't leave her that way, not even for one more night. But I'm finished now, and I'm sorry to have kept you so long. Time gets away from me when I'm focused on something, you know?"

"I do," Jensen said. Again, he almost laughed out loud. It was obvious the young woman thought he was a member of a maintenance crew or something.

"I could've sworn Paula told me you worked until long after nine tonight," she said as she turned and began to close whatever computer programs she'd been using to take the crack out of the face of the vintage bride. "I'm so sorry."

"It's fine," Jensen said as he strode into the room. "Can I see what you were working on?"

The young woman looked up to him, her blue eyes again flashing with the brilliance of sincerest excitement. "Oh, of course!" she exclaimed. Handing him the print of the photo, she said, "Isn't she gorgeous?" Jensen couldn't help but the grin then as the young lady sighed, "Just so classically beautiful, you know?"

"Yes," he agreed as he studied the photograph.

"Here…" she said, handing him a beat-up 8-by-10. "This is what had happened to her." The girl shook her head. "Can you believe it?"

The original photo was, indeed, very damaged. It had been bent vertically—almost looking as if it had been folded at one time—leaving a large, scarring crack in the finish that marred the bride's lovely face. There were flyspecks and foxing stains, and a bit of silvering as well. But as Jensen looked from the original photo to the restored version, he knew without any doubt that Paula had hired the right person for Wolfe Photography's photo restoration jobs.

"This is incredible," Jensen said aloud. "You've worked miracles on it."

"Not really," the young woman said. She frowned. "I always, always love the originals best, you know? Digital restorations just aren't the same to me." She shrugged. "But at least this lovely bride is restored for the family who brought the photo in. And I *do* like seeing her in all her unmarred glory."

As Jensen handed the print and original photo back to her, the young woman introduced herself. "I'm Valynn Wickley, by the way. The newest lucky duck to join the staff here."

She carefully deposited the photographs onto the desktop and offered a small, delicate-looking hand to Jensen. He was surprised with the strength of her grip when he accepted her handshake.

He couldn't help but grin a little more when he said, "Jensen Wolfe. Also one of the ducks lucky enough to be on staff here."

Valynn Wickley continued to smile her friendly smile—but only for a moment. As realization sunk in, the pretty blush on her cheeks that had pinked her up so endearingly before drained away completely, leaving her looking exactly as if she'd only just realized she stood face to face with the grim reaper.

"Sir, I am so sorry," Valynn started to apologize as her intestines began to twist themselves into knots of anxiety. "I had no idea who you were. I thought you…well, that you were here to lock up the building or something. I don't even know what I thought really…but I didn't think you were, you know, *you*."

Valynn found herself uncharacteristically breathless as Jensen Wolfe smiled down at her and said, "It's fine. Valynn? Is that right?"

"Yeah," she managed to answer.

"It's good to finally meet you," he said. "And your work is…" He shook his head with admiration. "Your work really is the best I've ever seen."

"Th-thank you! Wow, that means more than you can imagine…coming from you." she stammered.

Jensen Wolfe smiled, and Valynn thought, *Ay caramba! Who knew Jensen Wolfe was a giant-sized piece of eye candy?*

Instantly Valynn realized that she'd never really seen a photograph of the well-known photographer and entrepreneur. His work was so popular, as well as artistic, that she'd never paused to wonder what the man behind the camera looked like. But if she had taken a moment to wonder, she never, ever, ever would've imagined he was six foot three-ish, with gorgeous raven black hair, eyes that looked like two sapphires had been placed in them, the firmest, squarest, most perfectly shaped chin and jaw she'd ever seen on a man, and an overall appearance of just plain sigh-inducing hotness!

"Well, I'm just glad you agreed to work for us," Jensen said, still smiling at her. He glanced down at the original and restored photos lying on the desk. "That is incredible work. Really incredible."

"Thank you," Valynn managed. "And...I guess that's my cue to be on my way. I'm so sorry I'm here so late, sir. I just needed to finish, and Paula said it would be all right and—"

"It really is fine," Jensen assured her. "I don't like for people to have to work this late, but I understand. I would've felt the same way."

"Thank you," Valynn said, sighing with relief. When she'd realized who the man in the doorway really was, she'd worried that she might have overstepped her bounds somehow and endangered the job she'd worked so hard to get. But Jensen Wolfe didn't seem angry, so it looked like she was out of the woods.

"And please don't call me sir, okay?" he added.

"Okay, Mr. Wolfe," Valynn agreed as she began to gather her things.

She looked back up to him, however, when she heard a low chuckle.

"No, I mean, just call me Jensen. None of that sir or mister thing."

"Oh, okay. O-of course," Valynn stammered uncomfortably. She felt like his eyes were boring holes in the back of her head somehow! His gaze was so intense—so entirely unnerving—that she felt goose bumps prickling the back of her neck.

"Mind if I ask how old you are, Valynn?" Jensen asked then. "Just because I'm curious."

Valynn inhaled a deep breath, trying to push down the familiar agitation that normally rose inside her. She was young—she knew it—but she did a good job at what she did!

"Twenty, sir…um, I mean, Jensen," she answered.

Still, her defenses kicked in before she could stop them, and turning to face him once more, she asked, "How about you? How old are you? Just because I'm curious?"

Jensen Wolfe grinned—knowingly grinned—and answered, "Twenty-seven. And I *do* know how it feels to have people doubt your abilities just because you're young, Valynn. But I'm not one of those people, all right?"

Valynn blushed, embarrassed by her defensive attitude. "Is it that obvious?" she asked humbly.

Jensen grinned. "You mean the fact that you're super sensitive about people possibly judging your abilities by your age? Yeah…it is."

"Sorry," Valynn sighed. She wished she could get over it—the stupid sensitivity on the subject.

"Nothing to be sorry about," Jensen said, however. "I know how you feel. I've been there. But your work speaks for itself, so don't let anybody razz you about your age from here on out. I mean, not to sound cocky or anything," he smiled, "but you do work at Wolfe Photography, you know."

"Yes, I do," Valynn said, feeling suddenly quite proud of the fact she did indeed work for Wolfe Photography. "Thanks to you."

"Thanks to your work," he reminded her.

"Well, I guess I'm ready to leave for today," Valynn said. She glanced around to make sure she'd shut down everything that needed shutting down and put away everything that needed putting away. "Oh!" she exclaimed, realizing she hadn't put away the original old photograph of the beautiful Edwardian bride. Quickly she placed it back in the protective sleeve it had arrived in and then carefully slipped it into the desk drawer.

"Yeah, and I'm gonna be late for dinner if I don't get going," Jensen said. He offered her his hand and said, "Again, it was nice to finally meet you, Valynn. Have a good night."

"You too," Valynn said as she accepted his handshake. She glanced down, noting that even his hands were handsome! Especially where they connected to his strong, handsome wrists, which were attached to his beautifully sculpted, muscular forearms, which extended to his elbows and up over his incredible biceps!

She managed to find the courage to meet his mesmerizing gaze and return his dazzling smile as he let go of her hand and said, "See you later."

"Okay," she said, thinking her response sounded a little too breathy.

Jensen Wolfe began to turn and then paused and looked back at her. "Where are you parked? You know it's already dark, right?"

Valynn's heart fluttered with delight in the fact that he was enough of a gentleman to think of her well-being.

"Oh, just outside the back door," she answered. "Under the lamppost right there."

"I'll see you out," Jensen said, however, as he stepped aside to indicate she should exit the room ahead of him.

Valynn thought about arguing with him—giving him the typical response that she would be fine. But she thought better of it, for two reasons. First of all, she wanted him to walk her out—if only so she could study his gorgeousness a while longer. Second, she figured he was her boss and a man who didn't take no for an answer about certain things—like chivalry.

So instead of arguing with him, she simply said, "Thank you."

"You bet," Jensen said as he followed her down the corridor toward the back door of the building. "I have a thing about women leaving buildings alone…especially at night."

"Well, that's refreshing," Valynn told him. "Kind of a rare thing these days, you know."

It was small talk, but Valynn liked hearing his voice. It was strong and deeply resonated but also reassuring and soothing somehow.

They reached the back door of the building all too soon, and Jensen pushed the door open for her.

"Drive safely," he said.

"You too," Valynn returned. "And enjoy your dinner."

"I'll try," Jensen said, smiling at her one more time.

Valynn felt self-conscious as she walked the short distance to her car. She could feel him watching her, and it made her nervous. Once she'd opened her car door and the dome light illuminated the vehicle to prove no psychopaths were waiting in the back seat for her, she tossed a wave to the handsome Jensen Wolfe and sat down in the driver's seat.

She was amazed at the way he watched her until she started her car and began driving away before he closed the back door to the building and disappeared inside.

"Wow! What a gentleman!" she exclaimed out loud. "Who knew Jensen Wolfe of Wolfe Photography was so hot, hot, hot, hot, *hot*! Too hot for the hot tub, even!"

As she drove home, Valynn couldn't decide if she hoped Jensen would be around more at work or if she hoped he wouldn't. Having him around to admire would be awesome but also distracting. She couldn't have herself sitting around hoping to get a glimpse of him all day. And what if he were married? Then it would be entirely inappropriate for her gawk at him when he wasn't watching.

"*Ay caramba*," she sighed as she mulled the situation over in her mind. "It's a quandary, Valynn. A real quandary."

Still, Valynn sighed and tried to think of the excellent restoration she'd been able to perform on the Edwardian bride photo. It had turned out beautifully, and she was so glad. Maybe the family the original photo belonged to would have a large print framed of the bygone beauty and hang it somewhere in their home so she could always be remembered and admired. She hoped it would be the case. Furthermore, she hoped that Jensen Wolfe wasn't married. Then she wouldn't have to feel guilty in occasionally admiring his handsomeness. Or more than occasionally admiring it even.

After a quick shower and pulling on fresh clothes, Jensen headed for Le Porte Rouge—Rozlyn's favorite restaurant. Still, even as he was driving to meet her, Jensen kept wondering why—why was he meeting her?

He realized that he'd enjoyed less entertainment with Rozlyn in all their three weeks of dating combined than he'd experienced in the ten minutes he'd spoken with his new photo restorer in the computer room.

Jensen smiled as he thought of coming upon Valynn Wickley dancing her cute little booty off in front of the computer. He chuckled to himself, remembering how defensive she'd been when he asked her age. Yep! The girl was not only talented but amusing, as well. He had the feeling he'd get to have a few laughs at work at Valynn's expense, and the thought cheered him up.

It also *woke* him up! Why was he continuing to see Roz if he didn't even like her very much—didn't really enjoy her company? After all, wasn't that what dating was—a sorting out process in an effort to find someone he clicked with? And he certainly didn't click with Rozlyn. Jensen began to worry that maybe he was a shallow jerk like a lot of other guys, that maybe he was dating Rozlyn for the same reason he suspected she was dating him—because she looked good on his arm.

Suddenly, it was as if someone had smacked him on the back of his head, knocking some sense into him. Trying to ignore his growing self-disgust, he made the decision right then and there. As he pulled into a parking space in the parking lot of Le Porte Rouge, he determined that this would be his last dinner with Rozlyn Dawson—his last anything with Rozlyn Dawson.

As Jensen walked from his car to the fancy French restaurant's famous red door, he smiled as he thought of Valynn Wickley's verbal exclamation when she first saw the printed version of the photograph restored.

"*Ay caramba*? Who says *that*?" he chuckled to himself.

♥

"I mean, you should've seen this guy, Jensen!" Rozlyn exclaimed in a whisper. "He was so ripped! Abs of steel, a chest like a Greek god, you know?"

Jensen slowly nodded. He'd decided to wait until after they'd finished their meal to tell Rozlyn he wouldn't be going out with her anymore. But now, as she sat listing off the many fabulous attributes owned by the guy she'd done a photo shoot with earlier in the day, he wondered why he'd waited. It seemed clear that he'd rather have eaten by himself. For one thing, he'd have had time to think and relax. And for another, what kind of woman went on and on about some other guy when a guy she was supposed to be interested in was sitting right across from her? What? Jensen's abs weren't steely enough for Rozlyn's taste?

"Are you even listening to me, Jensen?" Jensen heard Rozlyn asked him.

He nodded. "Sure, Roz. I'm sitting here trying to listen to you talk about how hot some other guy is. It's a real exhilarating conversation."

"Oh, don't be like that, Jensen," Rozyln playfully scolded. "I wasn't saying he's hotter than you." She shrugged, adding, "Just that he's hot."

"Well, I'm glad you've got him then," Jensen said. He was tired of pussy-footing around. "Because I'm finished with this."

Rozlyn frowned. "You don't even want to get dessert?" she asked.

Jensen shook his head. "No, I mean I'm finished with this," he explained, gesturing between the two of them with one hand. "I'm finished with whatever this thing with me and you is. Actually, it's not much—almost nothing—and I'm done."

"You're breaking up with me?" Rozlyn exclaimed rather loudly then.

Jensen didn't even care that the other patrons of the restaurant ceased in their own individual conversations long enough to stare at Rozyln and him for a moment.

"I don't know if it's breaking up really," he began. "I'm not sure we were ever exclusive...or even really liked each other all that much. Are you?"

Rozlyn's brows furrowed with fury. "Well, how would we ever know if we liked each other or not, Jensen?" she growled in a lowered voice. "We've never once slept together! How are we supposed to know if we're a good match if we never even get to second base, hmmm?"

Jensen gritted his teeth with attempting to stay calm.

"Casual sex? That's second base to you, hmm?" he asked.

Rozlyn's beautiful eyebrows arched with astonishment. "Well, yeah. What's second base to you?"

"Damn, girl," Jensen almost chuckled. "I'd hate to know what you consider a home run."

"Now you're just being mean, Jensen," Rozlyn pouted.

Normally nothing could induce him into not being as gentlemanly as possible—but Rozlyn had. He removed his wallet from his back pocket and dropped two one-hundred dollar bills on the table. "That should cover the meal and the tip," he grumbled. He glared at Rozlyn and said, "And you've got your own car...so you'll get home all right." He pushed his chair back away from the table and stood up. "Have a good night, Rozlyn."

Jensen turned and strode from the restaurant. He didn't care what some of the other people in the restaurant thought of their conversation, and no doubt there had been eavesdroppers all along.

And he didn't care if the other men in the place thought he was insane for kicking an easy conquest to the curb. The moment he stepped out of Le Porte Rouge, Jensen Wolfe felt liberated. He swore he could breathe easier and that the very air smelled better.

"What the hell was I even thinking in the first place?" he exclaimed aloud.

But Jensen figured he could beat himself another time. He felt more alive, more relaxed, more positive about…well, everything.

He was finished with Rozlyn, and the knowledge invigorated him so much, he decided to stop and take a few timed exposures of the city lights on the way home. He knew the night air and the beauty of the city's lights gleaming like a trove of jewels beneath the dark sky would invigorate him.

"*Ay caramba*! Best after dinner conversation I ever had with Rozlyn," he chuckled to himself as he drove.

CHAPTER THREE

"So when were you gonna tell me that this new photo restoration girl was a pretty young thing, huh, Paula?" Jensen asked as he stepped into Paula's office, closing the door behind him.

Paula gulped a little guiltily. "Well, you said her work was great, so I didn't think it mattered that she was young," she explained.

"Young and *pretty*," Jensen corrected. He smiled then, and Paula sighed—relieved to know he was just teasing her.

"I'm guessing you finally met our Miss Valynn Wickley then, hmmm?" she asked.

"Oh, I met her all right," Jensen said, smiling. "I stopped by last night before meeting Rozlyn for dinner."

Paula's eyes narrowed with suspicion. Over the past few years of working for him, she'd learned to read Jensen Wolfe's smiles, and this smile was one she hadn't seen all that frequently. This was a smile of amusement *and* approval.

Still, Paula knew better than to press the matter too far, so she slickly changed the subject. "And how *was* your dinner with Rozlyn last night?" she asked. Secretly, she hoped it was horrible! Paula couldn't stand Rozlyn Dawson, and she couldn't figure out why it was taking Jensen so long to realize what a piece of work the woman was.

"It was great," Jensen answered. "In fact, it was the best date I've ever had with her."

Paula exhaled a quiet sigh of disappointment. "Well, that's nice," she mumbled begrudgingly.

"Yep," Jensen continued. "And you wanna know why it was the best one?"

A mild sort of trepidation began to well inside Paula. She loved Jensen Wolfe like a nephew or a little brother, and she hated to see him getting mixed up with a woman the likes of Rozlyn.

But just as Paula's imagination began to concoct all kinds of unsettling reasons, Jensen smiled and put her out of her misery by confessing, "Because it was my *last* date with her."

"It was?" Paula exclaimed far too gleefully.

Jensen laughed. "Yes, it was," he admitted. He quirked one eyebrow, stared at Paula, and asked, "Why the hell didn't you tell me what a waste of time *that* chick was?"

Paula exhaled a very heavy breath of relief then, shaking her head. "I try not to mix in with your personal life, Jensen. You know that," she reminded him.

"Saving my butt from embarrassment and a catastrophic waste of time, not to mention feeling like a gigolo, isn't mixing in. It's your responsibility as my friend, Paula," he teased her. He smiled one of his I-really-care-for-you-and-value-your-opinion smiles, and Paula felt blessed that he would donate one to her.

"Well, you make sure you remember that you just gave me permission to mix into it, Jensen," Paula giggled. "Therefore, that's the last time I let you be seen with a gold-digging dingbat on your arm."

"Is that a promise?" Jensen chuckled.

"It certainly is," Paula assured him.

And with that subject of conversation at an end, Paula felt that it would be perfectly appropriate to return to the previous topic.

"So?" she tentatively began. "What did you think of Valynn?"

Paula was pleased to see the amused admiration smile return to Jensen's handsome face.

"She sure is good at what she does," he answered. "She was finishing up a project last night when I stopped by."

"The beautiful, bent-up bride project?" Paula offered.

She couldn't help but think of the way Valynn had instantly fallen in love with the photo Paula had handed her the day before, exclaiming, "Oh, what a beautiful bride! She's a little bent up, but we can certainly fix that, now can't we?"

"Yeah," Jensen affirmed. "She did a heck of a job on it. She showed me the finished project last night."

"She was still here working that late?" Paula asked. "I mean, I told her she could stay after hours, but I had no idea she meant to finish it."

"Yeah, she was still here when I stopped by at seven," Jensen said, smiling as he thought back on his first vision of Valynn Wickley the night before. "And dancing around like a high school cheerleader at the same time."

"Multitasking," Paula said, nodding with amused approval. "Good to know she can do that."

"Yep," Jensen agreed. "She thought I was part of the maintenance crew." He laughed out loud then, adding, "You should've seen her eyes bug out when she figured out who I was."

"Oh, I can imagine," Paula laughed as well. Paula knew that Valynn's eyes had bugged out not only because she'd unexpectedly met the boss the night before but also because the boss was so unsettlingly attractive.

"Anyway," Jensen said, sighing as his laughter subsided, "you were right on the nose with hiring her, Paula. Thanks."

"Well, I'm glad you approve," Paula offered. "I can see that she'll be a real asset to the company. She's multitalented and a breath of fresh air when it comes to personality."

Jensen nodded. "She sure is," he mumbled, grinning to himself.

Paula liked the expression on Jensen's face right then. It gave her hope. The poor man hadn't had a decent girlfriend, in all the years Paula had known him, anyway. It seemed as if Jensen's rare good looks attracted the worst sort of women—self-centered, conceited, shallow women, who, though very beautiful physically, didn't have an ounce of real intelligence, compassion, or kindness in their stone-cold and often times lustful hearts.

In fact, it disturbed Paula, knowing that there were so many women who thought a solid, monogamous relationship was too much work or no fun—or that having a husband and children—a family—was an old-fashioned, chauvinistic ideal. And it caused her to carry a great burden of pity and worry when it came to Jensen, for he was a man of conviction and strength of character, mind, and body, a man who had so much more to offer to a woman than any other man of her current acquaintance.

If the full truth be told, it wasn't just Valynn Wickley's incredible talent with restoring photographs that made her the best person for the job at Wolfe Photography; it was also because Paula recognized that Valynn owned rare and wonderful qualities of character and a vibrant, happy personality that perfectly complemented the sort of man Jensen was. Certainly Paula knew Valynn was the supreme choice for the position at the company based on her skills alone; she would've hired her regardless. Still, Paula wouldn't lie to herself: she knew that in the most secret part of her heart, she'd hired Valynn in hopes that she would catch Jensen's eye, make him see that there were women far different from the Rozlyn Dawsons he was used to. And from the grin on her boss's face at that moment, Paula knew she'd done the right thing—all the way around.

"Excuse me? Mr. Wolfe?" Valynn said from the doorway of Paula's office then.

"Good morning, Valynn," Paula greeted.

"Good morning, Paula," Valynn returned, smiling and blushing a bit as Jensen nodded to her.

"What can I do for you?" Jensen Wolfe asked, smiling at Valynn and causing her breath to catch in her throat. *Ay caramba*, he was handsome! Valynn could swear her knees began knocking with the tiny fireworks of delight that began to travel through her veins.

"I, um…I wanted to apologize for last night," she began. The fact was that Valynn had spent a very restless night once she'd gotten home from work. She couldn't believe she'd thought Jensen Wolfe was someone other than Jensen Wolfe. Heck! His good looks and bulging muscles alone should have tipped her off to the fact that he was someone other than the night crew—like a male model arriving to look at shoot proofs or something. But no, Valynn had been too lost in the pleasure of how well her restoration of the bent-up bride had gone to think rationally when she'd turned to see him standing behind her—watching her.

Her restless night had also included wave after wave of relived humiliation when she began to wonder how long Jensen Wolfe, her boss, had been standing in the doorway watching her. Suffice it to be said, she hadn't slept but a few winks. Furthermore, she'd decided that an apology to her boss was in order—an apology for being such a dweeb at their first meeting. Thus, there she was—standing face-to-face with him, having embarked on her well-thought-out apology.

But when Jensen Wolfe frowned a little and asked, "Apologize for what?" Valynn felt as if her brain had dissolved into soup.

"Um...um...for...for being here so late and not knowing you were the...you know, my...the..." she stammered.

"The boss?" Paula suggested.

"Yeah," Valynn admitted with a sigh of relief. "I just didn't know it was you, and I feel...well, mortified, actually, that you arrived just as I was...um...finishing up my project."

"Oh, you mean because I arrived during your celebration?" he asked. There was a glint in his gorgeous blue eyes that hinted to Valynn he was the teasing type.

"Yes, sir," she admitted, relieved—for she could tell that he wasn't angry about the incident—not at all.

Jensen shrugged. "You did an awesome job on that restoration," he told her. He grinned again then, adding, "And the way I see it, you deserved to, you know, shake your groove thing a bit. Everybody has their own way of celebrating a job well done." He pointed to Paula, and as Valynn's mouth still gaped open a bit at his *shake your groove thing* remark, he said, "Take Paula, for example. Whenever she finishes up a good photo shoot, she hops in her car, heads out to the nearest mall parking lot, and accelerates to eighty-eight miles per hour…just to see if anything happens."

"Really?" Valynn asked. It sounded ridiculous, of course, but having only known Paula one week, she knew anything was possible.

"No, of course not," Paula giggled, slapping Jensen on one very sold arm. "Although I was in love with Michael J. Fox when I was younger, and Jensen is just bugged that I'm a bigger *Back to the Future* fan than he is."

"Except that you're not," Jensen playfully argued.

"Except that I am," Paula countered.

"Anyway," Jensen said, conceding victory. "The point is, you did a great job on that bride photo. So great, in fact, that I'd like to give you a little project of my own, if you don't mind. Something I'd like you to show at our gallery night. You can submit your own projects as well, but if you do as good a job on this one as I think you're going to do, heads will start spinning in admiration of your skills."

"Your gallery night?" Valynn asked, curious.

"Yep," Jensen said. "Twice a year I host a Wolfe Photography gallery night. Everyone here contributes. It's our chance to display some of our best work, and most of the time everyone sells every piece they present—the original custom-framed piece and prints of the same. You'll be contributing your own shots, I'm sure, but I'd really like to use the event as a springboard to show what can be done in the restoration area of things. Besides, a lot of the time, people who value awesome photographs really love nostalgic prints too. So I thought you and I could go through some of the ones in my personal collection—choose three or four that you think you can really do some awesome restoration on and that will present well as frameable print art, and see how the gallery guests respond."

"Really?" Valynn exclaimed as waves of excitement rose in her. "That would be fabulous! Do you really think people would be interested in prints of restored photographs?"

Jensen smiled, and the sight made Valynn tingle all over. He was so incredibly gorgeous!

"Absolutely," Jensen assured her. He shrugged. "I mean, I display antique photos in *my* home. They're awesome. So why wouldn't that appeal to other people?"

"I use them in my home too," Valynn chirped. It was her turn to shrug then, and she added, "I mean, I display them in my mom and dad's house, anyway. They kind of doubted they would like it when I first suggested it when I was a kid, but they love the ones they have now. It's probably a good thing I'm not rich; otherwise their whole house would look like a photo gallery instead of a home."

Again Jensen smiled, and again Valynn was afraid her knees might turn to pudding because it was so magnificent to witness.

"So, yeah, if you want to come with me for a few minutes, you can look through some stuff I have here at the office to see if there's anything that strikes your fancy for some restoration projects," he said. "Paula can dish you the dirt on our custom framing services. We pay for that for the gallery night. Anything you decide to contribute you can matte and frame here, and we pay the cost."

Valynn was almost certain that if she tried, she could take flight! The chance to display her restoration work at *any* event was something she'd only dreamt of before. But to display it alongside work promoted by Wolfe Photography—maybe even Jensen Wolfe himself—was incredible!

"And you do want Valynn to contribute original work too, right?" Paula asked.

Valynn had been so mesmerized by Jensen's mere presence and gorgeousness that she felt bad when she realized she'd almost forgotten Paula was even in the room.

"Of course," Jensen said.

"You mean…you mean, like, stuff I've shot myself?" Valynn asked then. She wasn't the photographer Jensen Wolfe was—not even close! Therefore, her excitement was a bit squelched.

"You bet," Jensen assured her. "Everyone here contributes to the gallery night."

"Yeah, but…everyone here is a professional," Valynn pointed out.

Paula smiled, placed a comforting hand on Valynn's arm, and asked, "Have you ever been paid anything for taking a photograph, Valynn?"

Valynn shrugged. "Well, yeah," she admitted. "But only stuff that anyone could do—senior pictures for high schoolers, and, like, I sell photo notecards in a couple of local antique stores and restaurants. But that doesn't count."

"Of course it does," Jensen assured her. "How many people do you know who get paid anything at all for their photos?"

"Not very many," Valynn answered. She frowned a moment and then added, "None but me, I guess, actually."

"Exactly!" Paula exclaimed. "Just because you don't get paid what some of us get paid, or what Jensen gets paid, doesn't mean you're not a professional photographer."

"You don't get paid what I get paid *yet*," Jensen stipulated, smiling at Valynn again. "But I saw those shots tucked into the back of your portfolio, and you definitely are a professional. So I want you to contribute your original works as well as the restorations you choose to do. All right?"

Valynn wouldn't deny it to herself or anyone else: she was incredibly excited about showing her work at Jensen's gallery night. Thus, she giggled and said, "All right! I guess I'm in!"

"Oh, you're in, all right," Paula mumbled to herself, watching Jensen's smile broaden as he studied Valynn intently.

"Great," Jensen said. "As I said, if you've got a minute, I'll show you where I keep my old photos here at work, and you can start by going through them. If you don't find anything there…well, I've got an entire room filled with boxes and notebooks of them at my place. So I'm sure you can find something, Valynn."

Paula noted the way Valynn's eyes lit up like firecrackers as she looked at Jensen and contemplated the possibilities surrounding the old photographs. *That's it*, she thought to herself. *These two were made for each other!*

Paula had never known anyone who was in love with antique photographs the way Jensen was—until now. And beyond a mutual love for photography and photos of the past, Paula could see there was a mutual attraction passing between her boss and his newest employee that was about to set the room on fire! It was going to be fun to watch their courting dance, so to speak—she knew it!

"Valynn Wickley," Paula began.

"Yeah?" Valynn asked, tearing her gaze away from Jensen.

"I can see that hiring you was just about the best decision I've ever made," Paula answered.

"Well, I hope so," Valynn said.

"Come on," Jensen said, lightly slapping Valynn on one arm like she was an old army buddy. "I'll show you where I keep my old stuff here, so when you have time you can rummage through them, okay?

As I said, I've got one in particular I'd like for you to do for me, but I want you to choose the others for gallery night."

"This is going to be like Christmas morning!" Valynn exclaimed to Paula a moment before she followed Jensen out of the room.

"Oh, I have no doubt," Paula giggled.

♥

Jensen Wolfe's collection was breathtaking! Incredible! And as Valynn began carefully going through a box of antique photographs in the storage room Jensen had taken her to, she thought to herself that the moment really was as exciting as Christmas morning.

Every photograph in the box was a treasure! Photo after photo of Edwardian families, Victorian families, Civil War soldiers, children, couples, landscapes—it was a dream come true for someone who, like Valynn, loved historic photographs!

Of course, Valynn had her own collection of antique photos, but she could tell that if Jensen Wolfe had an entire room at his home filled with photographs the likes of the ones he had at the office building, her own photo collection was dwarfed by the size and quality of his.

Valynn paused in looking through the box of photos in her lap to pick up the photo Jensen had specifically requested she work on. She studied it carefully, delighted by the subject matter. The photograph was of a wonderfully nostalgic winter scene. Beautiful old buildings stood in the background, and streets covered in snow surrounded a park lined with tall, leafless oak tress. A community parade of some sort was the focus of the photograph. Young adolescent boys wearing knitted striped sweaters and long knitted stocking caps pulled toboggan-type sleds behind them. They preceded a team of six large mules pulling a beautiful parade float with the words *Carnival Queen* sewn into the skirting that hid the sleigh the float was built on.

A young woman draped entirely in fluffy, white furs sat atop a small throne at the back of the float, while a man wearing a heavy brown fur coat stood at the front of the float holding the lines to the team of mules.

More boys were at the back of the float and appeared to be helping it along by pushing it from behind. Each had a pair of snowshoes strapped to his back.

But for all the wonderment of the boys, sleds, float, and carnival queen in the foreground of the photograph, it was the background goings-on that most intrigued and delighted Valynn. Scattered here and there throughout the snowy streets behind the float and stocking-capped boys were several sleighs—one- or two-horse open sleighs—their occupants bundled in coats and hats of a beautiful bygone era.

Valynn was impressed by Jensen's dating the photo to the mid-late 1890s; she recognized the style of women's hats and the leg-o'-mutton sleeves as true to that time, but she was surprised at first that a guy would know it. Still, this guy collected vintage photographs, so she guessed it made sense he would be able to date them well.

The longer Valynn gazed at the photograph—studied the smiling faces of the children sitting on the park fence watching the parade and the lovely scene surrounding them—the more she fell in love with the image and the more she understood just why Jensen had chosen it, specifically, for her to restore. Not only was it a very rare sort of image of the time period but it also conveyed such a feeling of wonderment and nostalgia that Valynn doubted anyone could ever look at it and not feel a sense of appreciation and longing for the past.

The photograph itself was in pretty good shape too, marred only by light surface scratches and a few lousy flyspecks. It wouldn't be hard to clean it up, but Valynn was determined she would do much more than fix the physical signs of age to the photo. She would do her best to enhance the background of it as well.

"Oh, I can just imagine you all matted and framed up and hanging in a gallery!" Valynn exclaimed to herself. She smiled and quietly added, "Your owner has an eye for the best, that's for sure! A couple of beautiful, blue, dreamy eyes that make my knees weak, by the way."

Valynn giggled and then sighed with satisfaction as she laid the snowy parade scene aside and began carefully rummaging through the box of photographs in her lap once more. It truly was a treasure box—a treasure box filled with beautiful images of history and nostalgia. And she wondered for a moment if Jensen Wolfe's heartstrings were as sensitive as her own—or did he value the photographs simply for their photographic value?

CHAPTER FOUR

When Paula had mentioned to Valynn the following morning that Jensen wanted to take the entire staff to lunch that day so they could get to know Valynn, as apparently he did whenever a new person joined the staff at Wolfe Photography, Valynn had no idea just how big a deal the staff lunch would be!

The hoity-toity Italian restaurant—whose name Valynn couldn't even pronounce—had a special room for larger parties who still wished to have great, understandable conversation. It was a large round room with a big circular table in the very center of it. Apparently the domed-shaped ceiling created just the right conditions for conversation—meaning that no matter where a person sat at the round table, everyone else at the table could hear what was said. The incredible acoustics were one of the reasons Jensen always held employee lunches or dinner events at the restaurant—so Paula explained as she took a seat next to Valynn at the table that afternoon.

"Not to mention that the food is supreme here!" Paula whispered to Valynn.

Valynn was nervous. She'd met Paula and Jensen, of course, but the rest of the people taking their seats at the table were new to her. It was in that moment that she realized just how stealth she'd tried to be at her new job. Whether it was her worry over people judging her for her youthfulness or whether she'd just buried herself so entirely in her work so far that she hadn't looked up for a moment to see anyone, Valynn knew she needed to make a better effort to get to know her coworkers.

Once everyone was seated and two waiters had finished taking everyone's drink orders, Jensen began.

"Okay, so you guys all know we're here to welcome Valynn and get to know a little more about her, right?" Jensen said.

Everyone at the table nodded and smiled at Valynn. She could feel her cheeks blush pink with discomfort. She didn't like being the center of attention—not one bit.

"So, Valynn," Jensen said, looking at her from his place across the wide table from her, "what we usually do is go around the table and everyone tells you their name and what they do at the company. Okay?"

"Sure," Valynn said, "though I can't promise I'll remember everything right away," she added as she looked at the other thirteen people sitting at the table.

Everyone smiled with understanding, and she felt better.

"Of course not," Jensen reassured her. "It takes a while, especially with the likes of all of us. It seems like we're always preoccupied with something. Right?"

Everyone agreed with smiles and verbal remarks.

"So I'll start," Jensen began. "Then we'll go clockwise, okay?" Smiling at Valynn and causing her blush to intensify even further, he said, "I'm Jensen Wolfe, and I do, like, the big client photo shoots and stuff like that. I kind of am the manager, I guess."

"The manager?" a dark-haired woman to Jensen's right teased.

"Yeah," Jensen confirmed.

Valynn smiled. She liked the way Jensen tried not to put himself above his employees—created a feeling of equality among everyone there. She'd noticed it before and even talked about it with Paula, who confirmed it as one of the reasons everyone was so happy to work for Jensen.

"I'm John Hornberger, and I'm the lighting guy," a husky young man to Jensen's left announced. "Nice to have you on board, Valynn."

"Thank you," Valynn said, smiling at John. She could see he was a jolly guy and knew she didn't have to be afraid to talk to him.

"I'm Ruth," a middle-aged blonde woman said next. "I'm set design, props—you know, the stuff lady. We're glad to have you, Valynn."

"Thanks," Valynn said.

Several more employees introduced themselves: Becky Thompson, the makeup girl; Chris Shelton and Tim Russell, the printing guys; Desirae DiQuarto, the custom framing specialist; and Sunny Harden, the baby portrait maker.

Then it was Valynn's turn. "I'm Valynn Wickley," she began. Smiling, she added, "I'm guessing, by the way you all are introducing yourselves…that I'm Valynn, the old photo restorer or something, right?"

Everyone laughed but then, much to her surprise, began calling out titles of their own.

"How about Valynn, the hot chick photo fixer?" John suggested.

"Naw, she might sue me over that one," Jensen laughed.

"How about Valynn of the Restoration?" Becky offered.

"Hmmm…nope," Jensen said.

"How about just Valynn, the vintage photo fixer girl?" Paula suggested. "It's easier than saying restorer and won't get you sued for sexual harassment, Jensen."

Valynn laughed as Jensen nodded. "I like that one. Valynn, the vintage photo fixer girl, it is." He nodded to the man to Valynn's left then, saying, "Okay, let's keep going. Your turn, Mack."

Valynn looked to the tall, blond young man to her left as he said, "I'm Mack Farmer, the equipment dude."

"Nice to meet you, Mack," Valynn giggled.

Just the introductions were fun! After everyone had become known to her, she had a sense that working at Wolfe Photography was going to be even more wonderful than she had at first imagined.

Once everyone had placed orders and the appetizers arrived, Valynn was further delighted with the fact that the center of the table was one big lazy Susan. Jensen had ordered several different appetizers, and once everyone had taken something from the plate in front, he just rotated the lazy Susan table center, giving everyone a chance to sample everything.

"The portions here are huge!" Paula explained. "For instance," she continued, "you ordered the lasagna, right?"

"Yeah," Valynn confirmed.

"Well then, the waiters will bring an entire lasagna out, serve you, and then put the rest in the middle of the table. That way everyone can have exactly what they ordered but also taste everything everybody else ordered. It's so delicious! I always eat until I'm sick when Jensen brings us here."

"Wow!" Valynn exclaimed. "And all of this just because there's a new employee?"

"You bet!" Jensen answered from across the table.

Valynn understood then that, as wonderful as the acoustics were, it would be mighty difficult to have a private conversation if a body wanted to.

"New talent joining the firm is something to celebrate," Jensen elaborated. "And I don't know about you, Valynn, the vintage photo fixer girl, but the rest of us at Wolfe Photography love to eat!"

And he wasn't kidding! As the food arrived and began to be served, Valynn looked around at her fellow employees. They were having the time of their lives—and not only because of the incredible food. It was obvious to Valynn that these people really liked each other—sincerely enjoyed one another's company—and she began to wonder if a job really could be a passion instead of just a job.

Valynn always heard there were three kinds of employment: a job, something a person had to do to earn a living; a career, something someone chose to do to earn a living and enjoyed; and a passion, something someone chose to do, loved to do, and earned a living doing. The expressions on the faces of her fellow workmates, and just the general feeling of camaraderie among them, put Valynn to thinking that maybe, just maybe, she would be one of the lucky ones—someone who found they could make their living and love doing so.

Yet as often occurs in moments of zeal, something happened then—and it was the worst! Lost in her marvel of how happy everyone was, Valynn took a bite of garlic bread and swallowed too fast. Before she knew it, a crispy crust piece of garlic bread was making its way down, causing her severe discomfort—even mild pain—as it poked and stretched its way down her throat.

As Valynn began to cough—her eyes blurring with the tears of distress that accompany such an experience—she was mortified when she reached for her water glass to see that only ice cubes remained.

"Are you all right?" Paula asked.

Valynn nodded, coughing and fanning her face in a desperate attempt to cool her blush and diminish the moisture gathering in her eyes. "I just swallowed wrong, and it's killing me," she explained.

"Is she all right?" Valynn heard Jensen ask from across the round table. Everyone's conversation fell silent as they turned their attention to her, frowns of concern puckering their brows.

"I'm okay," Valynn choked. "I just need some water. I swallowed a piece of bread wrong and—" She couldn't explain further as a nasty cough overwhelmed her. She could tell the crispy bread crust was stuck! It felt like she'd swallowed the blade of an X-ACTO knife.

"Give her some water," Jensen rather demanded.

"It's okay," Valynn choked again. "I can breathe. It's just some garlic bread caught in my throat."

Quickly Paula handed her own glass of water to Valynn. "Here, have mine."

Valynn nodded, choked a quiet thank you, and took a big drink of the water. As the water dislodged the piece of garlic bread, she did begin to feel some relief.

"I'm so sorry," Valynn said. Her blushing now had nothing to do with the sharp garlic bread crust piece that had assaulted the lining of her esophagus but was strictly due to embarrassment. Everyone at the table was still staring at her with expressions of concern—especially Jensen.

"You have nothing to be sorry for," Jensen reminded her. "But are you okay now?"

Valynn took another sip of water and nodded. "Yes. I just swallowed something wrong, and it was stuck in my asparagus. I'm fine now."

Valynn didn't know what to think in the next instant, when everyone at the table who had been frowning a moment before looked to be fighting the urge to laugh.

"You're sure you're okay?" Jensen asked, chuckling as a broad smile stretched across his handsome face.

"Yes," Valynn assured him—curious at why he seemed amused.

It was Paula who lost it first, and as Paula began to laugh as if she'd just witnessed the most hysterical thing she'd ever seen in her life, Valynn frowned—for everyone else began to laugh as well.

"Did...did I miss something?" Valynn asked as Paula struggled to gain control of herself again. "I must've really looked goofy when I was choking, right?"

But Paula shook her head. "No...no, of course not, Valynn," she giggled, wiping tears of amusement from the corners of her eyes. "It's the way you said it—that something was stuck in your throat."

"Yeah? In my asparagus," Valynn said. But as everyone began roaring with laughter once more, realization washed over her. "I meant my esophagus, of course."

"We knew what you meant," one of the other ladies at the table assured her. "That's why it's so funny! You're adorable! I can see that you're really gonna brighten things up at work."

"No doubt," Jensen added, still chuckling.

"Well, now I feel like a total goober, that's for sure," Valynn said—even though she was laughing at herself by then. "My asparagus? What an idiot! I must've been panicking worse than I thought."

Jensen wondered if he'd ever be able to think of the word *asparagus* again without cracking up out loud. Valynn had totally meshed up his emotions—sending him into a near state of panic of concern for her safety when she began to choke while simultaneously activating his sense of humor when she referred to her esophagus as asparagus. Becky was right: things around the office promised to be even more interesting than before with Valynn on board.

Jensen smiled as he watched Valynn laughing with the others. It was amazing to him—the fact that she was able to laugh at herself the way she was doing, find amusement in the situation instead of getting her feelings hurt or faulting the others for finding theirs. It was a rare gift of character, being able to laugh at oneself—a personality trait that seemed to have vanished from a greater portion of the populace of late. It made Jensen admire Valynn all the more.

Of course, he reminded himself that he couldn't admire her too much. After all, he'd only known her, what? Twenty-four hours? Still, Valynn Wickley had captured his attention. Maybe it was simply because he'd met Valynn so closely to when he broke up with Rozlyn. But the contrast between the vintage photo fixer girl who now worked for him and Rozlyn, the faux piece of work he'd been dating, was like day and night!

As Jensen sat listening to the friendly, upbeat conversation transpiring between all those who worked for him—those he also considered friends—his gaze caught Paula's for a moment.

Good hire, Jensen mouthed to Paula in silence.

Winking at him, Paula smiled and mouthed, *I know*, in return.

"So? Is there anything you don't like about restoration work?" Jensen heard John ask Valynn.

The question immediately drew Jensen's attention back to Valynn—because he was more than just a little interested in her answer himself.

"Yep," Valynn admitted to John.

"And what might that be?" Tim asked.

"Flyspecks. I hate flyspecks!" Valynn answered.

Jensen and Paula exchanged amused glances, and Jensen didn't feel so bad, knowing that Paula was as entertained as he was by Valynn's response.

"Are they difficult to digitally remove or something?" Becky asked.

Valynn sighed, shaking her head. "No," she admitted. "Sometimes I can even flake them off with my fingernail or a soft eraser before I scan the original to a digital format. It just makes me mad that flies poop on pictures, you know?"

"Well, this sounds like a very promising explanation indeed," John chuckled quietly aside to Jensen.

"I mean, it's sickening!" Valynn began as she launched into a small tangent. "Flies sick me out anyway, and having to scrape their poo off a beautiful photograph just angers me, you know?"

"I can see why," Jensen said, trying very hard not to smile. He couldn't, of course, but he also couldn't wait to hear all she had to say about her obvious loathing for flies.

"And don't get me started on how they eat!" Valynn exclaimed.

"Oh, I'm sure," Paula giggled.

But Valynn was too far gone on her fly tangent to stop now. Waging an index finger at first Paula and then John, she asked, "You know how they eat, don't you?"

"Not really," John admitted.

"Well," Valynn began, her detest for the buzzing bug that left spots on old photographs obviously mounting, "they vomit on what they're going to eat so that their digestive juices break down whatever it is into this slurpable gunk so they can slurp it back up through this straw-like thing they have as part of their mouth. I think it's called a proboscis or something. Is that sick or what? I mean, think about it. If you're at a birthday party, and you look over and see a fly sitting on top of the cake, it's throwing up on it so it can slurp the slurpable stuff up through its straw thingy! So what if you see the fly, and it's already thrown up on the cake, and then you shoo it away before it had time to slurp up the gunk? And then what if the hostess of the birthday party is serving cake and you get that exact piece of cake with the fly vomit juice on it?"

Jensen and the rest of the men at the table laughed when Valynn and the other women simultaneously gagged a little.

"And then, if that isn't bad enough," Valynn continued, "the stinking fly zooms into the other room and poos on your family photographs." She paused, exhaling a heavy breath as she sighed, "I hate flies."

"I think we're getting that," Jensen offered, unable to keep from smiling. It was obvious Valynn Wickley was a scream when she was worked up. Jensen made a mental note to himself—a reminder that he needed to get her worked up more often. If all her rants were as entertaining as this one on houseflies, he was definitely going to have to play on that!

Exhaling another heavy sigh as she began to settle down, Valynn said, "It's why I'm not sure I could ever live on a farm. Way too many flies around to be barfing on birthday cakes and pooing on pictures, you know?"

And that was it—the straw that broke the backs of all the camels in the room who had been trying so hard not to laugh at, or with, Valynn again.

"Jensen…this chick is going to be hysterical to have around, man!" John told Jensen.

"Yeah," Jensen said, chuckling as he watched Valynn take a bite of her lasagna. "I'm beginning to see that more and more."

"Awesome hire, dude! Seriously!" John laughed.

"Thank Paula, man," Jensen said. He firmly believed in giving credit where credit was due. "She's the one who discovered her."

Jensen made another mental note to himself—to thank Paula again for having such a great way of finding just the right person to work at Wolfe. He figured a thousand dollars tucked into her wallet when she wasn't looking might do it.

"Geez!" he heard someone say. "I'll never look at flies the same way again."

"Or birthday cake," someone else said.

Returning the smile Valynn offered to him when she looked up and caught him staring at her, Jensen also nodded with approval. He saw the young woman visibly sigh with relief, and he could see that she believed she just might fit in at Wolfe Photography with the rest of them—and he was glad.

♥

"So?" Paula asked as she stepped into the storage room.

After lunch, Valynn had finished the restoration projects she'd had pending for the day and then returned to the storage room to rummage through some more boxes of old photos.

"Any luck?" Paula asked as she sat down in a chair next to Valynn.

Valynn shook her head with feeling overwhelmed. "It's like walking into a cave full of treasure and being told to pick the most beautiful gem!" she sighed.

Resting her arms on the table before them for a moment, Paula smiled when she picked up the photo of the winter parade scene Jensen had asked Valynn to restore. "Oh, I've always loved this one, ever since Jensen found it at a garage sale a couple of years ago."

"A garage sale? Are you kidding me?" Valynn exclaimed in utter astonishment. "Someone put this in a garage sale?"

"Yep," Paula assured her.

Valynn shook her head. "That's a travesty, you know?"

"Wait until I tell you what he paid for it," Paula said.

"What?" Valynn asked.

"Fifty cents," Paula stated.

"Are you even kidding me?" Valynn again exclaimed. "Why…why, it's probably worth—I don't know—one hundred dollars on the antique market!"

"I know," Paula agreed. "Jensen said it was stuffed in a big box full of old fading Polaroid shots and stuff."

Valynn sighed with sadness. "I'm sure the story behind it just got lost over the generations, being that there's no description on the back. And whoever ended up with it just didn't realize its value."

"That's exactly what Jensen said," Paula mentioned as she returned the photo to its place on the table. "And what did you think of lunch today, hmm?"

Immediately Valynn's mood lightened. "It was wonderful! Everyone here is so kind and friendly." She winked at Paula, lowering her voice and adding, "I guess I can quit skulking around the hall trying to avoid anyone. They all seem so welcoming that I don't know what I was afraid of."

"Everyone is nice and really great to work with," Paula said. "And I heard you had quite the first meeting with Jensen last night, hmm?"

"Oh my gosh! That was so embarrassing!" Valynn laughed. "Did he tell you that I thought he was, like, a maintenance guy or something?"

Paula laughed too. "Yeah, he did."

"I mean," Valynn began, "I didn't realize anyone else was still here, and then I turned around, and holy guacamole! Mr. Gorgeousness was standing right behind me, all beefed up and stuff. I think he had been working out."

"Probably," Paula agreed.

"I mean, I don't know if you've noticed, Paula, but Jensen Wolfe is, like, *beautiful*! Do you know what I mean?" Valynn babbled in a lowered voice. "No wonder he flies so far under the radar—never having his picture included with articles and stuff, you know? And I totally can't believe he's not married yet. At least, I assume he's not, you know, being that he doesn't wear a wedding ring and stuff…though I guess he could be one of those guys who just doesn't wear a wedding ring. But he seems like he would, if he were married."

"You're right. He's not married," Paula affirmed. "And yes, we've all noticed how *beautiful* Jensen is."

"In my day, we would've called him a total sexy beast, you know?" Valynn added with a giggle.

"In my day, we would've called him a total fox," Paula offered.

Valynn smiled at Paula. Sighing with gratitude, she said, "Thank you so much for this opportunity, Paula. It's my dream job, you know?"

"Thank you for taking the job, Valynn," Paula said. "And I think you'll find that not only is this your dream job but Jensen Wolfe is your dream boss."

Again Valynn giggled. "Oh, I hear that," she said. "He knows what he's doing in this business. That's obvious. And I could spend years going through his photo collection. Not to mention I'll probably have blisters on my eyeballs from gawking at him. *Ay caramba*!"

Paula was simply enchanted by Valynn's honesty. She seemed to be a no-holds-barred type of person—yet with a great deal of tact and decorum when necessary. Paula was looking forward to working with Valynn on photographic projects and was curious to see what her talents and skills would bring to the company. But what Paula most looked forward to was seeing what might happen between Valynn and Jensen.

It was obvious from the way she talked so openly about Jensen that Valynn had not one thought or hope in the world that Jensen might actually be interested in her for any reason other than what she could bring to his firm. Valynn saw Jensen as a beautiful poster-boy dream man—not as a potential suitor, or more.

Furthermore, Paula knew Jensen himself hadn't realized how big his smile had been each time Valynn had been in the same room with him that day. And *that* was why Paula knew she was about to be entertained to the gills—for she was certain something wonderful was about to begin at Wolfe Photography.

CHAPTER FIVE

"Good morning, Valynn," Vickie, the receptionist, greeted her with a sincere and friendly smile.

It had been a month since Valynn had started working at Wolfe Photography, and she smiled as she entered the reception area that morning on her way to her office.

"Good morning, Vickie," Valynn greeted in return. "Any exciting news this morning?"

"Well, actually, yes," Vickie answered.

"Really?" Valynn asked, stopping in her tracks in front of Vickie's desk.

"Yeah," Vickie said. Lowering her voice, she continued, "You've heard of Brian Collins—the lead singer of that rock band, the Jones Experiment?"

"Yeah?" Valynn prodded.

"Well, I guess Brian Collins is going to do a solo album or CD or whatever it's called now that everything is digital. And he wants Jensen to shoot the photos for the cover and PR stuff!"

"Wow!" Valynn exclaimed. "That's huge, right?"

Vickie nodded emphatically. "Way huge! Like upwards of ten grand!"

"Seriously?" Valynn asked.

"Yep…for one shoot," Vickie said. "I think it's because Jensen doesn't enjoy working with celebrities on any level. So he's making sure it's worth his time and talent, you know?"

"I can imagine," Valynn said. "I've heard that guy is a jerk."

"Yeah," Vickie agreed. She brushed a stray strand of dark brown hair from her cheek, adding, "I actually think Jensen was trying to price himself out of doing the shoot, but Brian Collins's manager went for it."

"So when is the shoot scheduled?" Valynn asked. "I'd love to be a bug on the wall to witness Jensen in action. I still haven't gotten to assist on any shoots around here. I've been too busy."

"Which is good, right?" Vickie teased. "So much work that you've instantly become invaluable to the company!"

Valynn smiled and nodded. "Job security is a good thing," she admitted. "But I would love to see Jensen in his element, you know?"

"Oh, you'll get your chance," Vickie assured her. "It gets really busy around here starting this time of year. Everybody ends up assisting Jensen at one time or another…even me!"

"Good," Valynn sighed. "I think I could learn a lot from him."

"Oh yeah! He really is the best around, you know?" Vickie commented. She tipped her head to one side then, and her brows puckered with curiosity. "Have you got your gallery pieces all worked out?"

"I do," Valynn said, nodding her assurance. "I kind of had to work fast. I didn't realize when Jensen told me about it just how close the gallery night actually was! Only another couple of weeks to get everything framed and stuff. But I'll make it."

"I heard the restoration pieces you're doing are fabulous!" Vickie said. "At least, that's what Jensen told me. He says you really chose some incredible photographs to restore."

"I hope so," Valynn admitted. "I worry. I want to make him happy with the finished product."

"Oh, you will," Vickie encouraged, offering another friendly smile. She touched her headset then and whispered, "Gotta go. I'm getting a call. See you later, Valynn."

"You too," Valynn whispered.

"Brian Collins, hm?" Valynn mumbled to herself as she hurried to her office. "It never gets dull around here, that's for sure."

If working with Jensen for a month had taught her anything, it was that he was very picky about certain types of shoots. Although Jensen Wolfe was incredible with any subject he was photographing, Valynn knew he preferred to shoot portraits of individuals rather than enormous groups. She knew he loved to photograph elderly people, especially in black and white. She knew he enjoyed shooting old buildings, especially abandoned houses. Valynn knew that when it came to pets included in family photographs, Jensen preferred dogs to cats. She'd heard him tell John once that dogs looked like they were smiling most of the time, but cats just looked like they were bored divas in still photographs.

Yep! Valynn had learned a ton about Jensen Wolfe—his habits, preferences, likes, and dislikes. And all of it she'd learned from intense, though stealth, observance of him whenever she was with him. Deliciously, she'd found herself spending quite a bit of time with Jensen—at least an hour or so day.

For one thing, the restoration department at Wolfe Photography had exploded about ten days after Valynn arrived. Jensen had done an incredible job promoting his firm's now offered restoration services, and the examples from Valynn's portfolio that she'd allowed to be uploaded to the Wolfe Photography website had really grabbed the attention of many of Jensen's clients. Valynn was relieved, of course—feeling great about pulling in good money for Jensen and his company. But it also helped to boost her self-confidence, not to mention offering challenges that she loved to triumph above.

However, Valynn had quickly discovered that the most wonderful, the most incredible, the most marvelous part of working at Wolfe was Jensen himself! Oh sure, he was gorgeous, kind, smart, talented, and a very wise businessman. But Valynn had quickly discovered that Jensen was also as passionate about his work as Valynn was about hers, that he owned a fabulous wit and sense of humor, and that he was just basically a total heartthrob all the way around!

It was true, and Valynn could admit it to herself—though she would never admit it to anyone else. She was pretty much manically attracted to Jensen Wolfe; she dreamt about him every night, daydreamed about him for a significant portion of the day, and secretly wished that he would fall in love with her, sweep her off her feet, and carry her away to a lifetime of wedded bliss, children, and happiness. Nevertheless, being a goober who was head-over-heels in love with her boss didn't mean she was ignorant enough to actually *believe* anything could ever really happen between them. He was Jensen Wolfe, after all—beef-cake-ily beautiful, years older than she, far more talented, far more experienced, far more accomplished in his trade than she was, and just plain out-of-reach for a girl who simply liked to take photographs, restore old pictures, and dream of someday being the throwback traditional housewife and mommy.

Still, Valynn wasn't unhappy that she had promptly fallen in love with her boss. She wasn't miserable—at least not yet. Instead, she chose to enjoy being in Jensen's presence—to enjoy the dreaming about him—to enjoy everything about being around him while she could. And so she did.

Furthermore, she was pretty sure he enjoyed her. Valynn couldn't count the times over the few weeks that Paula had told her she'd never seen Jensen laugh the way he laughed when Valynn said something that amused him. Of course, the asparagus incident of her welcome lunch had quickly turned to legend among everyone at the office. And Valynn didn't mind at all—especially when Jensen would periodically smile, begin chuckling, and mumble, "My asparagus," under his breath when they were working together. She figured she'd managed to make him happy—leave him with an amusing memory that brightened his day every time he thought of it—and, after all, that was something. Maybe it wasn't being held in his arms as he smothered her with passionate kisses, but at least he'd think of her anytime he saw asparagus for the rest of his life.

"Oh, you're gonna love this one!" Jensen said as he stepped into Valynn's office.

Instantly Valynn's heart and mood soared all the way up to cloud nine as she turned to look at him.

She saw that he was holding several large, brownish antique photo folders.

"Edwardian?" she asked with rising excitement.

"Yep," Jensen confirmed, his handsome smile broadening.

"Wedding?" Valynn inquired.

"Absolutely," Jensen again confirmed.

"Awesome! My favorite!" Valynn squealed, clasping her hands together with delight and anticipation.

"I know," Jensen chuckled.

Over the past few weeks Jensen had discovered that Edwardian wedding photos were Valynn's favorite type of antique photos to work on. She'd once told him she found the bridal attire, prolific flower arrangements, and occasional little kids beautifully fascinating. He'd found that he'd paid a bit more attention to the genre of photographs after that—and that they were incredible.

"But that's not all, my vintage photo fixer girl," he said as he handed the set of photographs in folders to her.

"What is it?" Valynn asked.

The brilliant excitement in her bright blue eyes caused Jensen to chuckle again. "You'll see," he teased.

"Are there kids in these?" Valynn began to guess as she carefully placed the photographs on her desk and began to open one. "A bridesmaid with a shepherdess hook?"

"Nope," Jensen answered.

But when Valynn opened the first folder and squealed, "Smiles!" Jensen knew she was pleased. "Smiles! The bride *and* the groom are smiling!" she squealed again. "Smiles on people being photographed in this era are so hard to find."

"Yes, ma'am," Jensen said. "And they're a set—bridal portrait, bride and groom, and wedding party…all with the same subjects."

"No way!" Valynn exclaimed in awe. "Who brought them in?"

"They're mine," Jensen answered.

"Yours?" Valynn gasped.

"Yep," he said. "I'd forgotten all about them. But when you showed up at Wolfe and I figured out that these were some of your favorite types of photos…well, I knew I had them stuck somewhere in a box. So last night I dug around until I found them. They're in pretty bad shape, but if you want to add them to the restoration stuff for the gallery night—I mean, if you think you have time—I think they'd be a real conversation piece."

"Are you serious?" Valynn asked.

Jensen could see the excitement welling in her, and it caused a sense of elation to mount in his chest. He'd discovered that there was nothing more amazing than the expression on Valynn Wickley's face when she was delighted about something or really, really amused. And the photographs he'd brought to her had had exactly the effect on her he'd hoped: utter delight.

"Of course I'm serious," Jensen assured her. "I mean, you've put a lot of work into pieces for gallery night already. So if you think it's too much—"

"It's not too much," she interrupted him, giggling with anticipation. "And you're right. These will make a beautiful arrangement. Thank you for finding them! I love them already."

"I figured you would."

Jensen didn't want to leave Valynn's office. He wanted to linger in her company all day long. But he'd only had the one reason—delivering the photographs to her—as an excuse to drop in on her at all, and that ship had sailed far faster than he would've liked.

But, it *had* sailed, so he took one last soul-quenching look at her pretty, elated face and expression and said, "Well, let me know if you need help with anything you're working on, okay?"

"Oh, I will," Valynn answered.

"Have fun with them," Jensen said.

"Thank you so much, Jensen," she said to him as he turned to leave.

"You bet," he called over his shoulder.

Stepping out into the hallway, Jensen exhaled a heavy sigh. Valynn Wickley had him completely wrapped around her little finger, and she didn't even know it! But what could he do? He was her boss, after all. Any heavy flirting to tip her off to the way he felt about her might be misconstrued as sexual harassment, either by Valynn herself or Jensen's other employees. And as a man in business for himself, Jensen knew to steer clear of anything that even resembled it. Not that anyone who worked for him would accuse him of it—or at least he hoped no one would—but it was a risk.

And yet sometimes Jensen wondered if he were simply scared of rejection. Chicks like Rozlyn were a dime a dozen; he'd come to know that the hard way. Plus, he'd had it reaffirmed every time he had a conversation with Valynn. Women like Valynn were rare, and who was he but a guy that had never managed to have a serious, lasting relationship with a girl, ever? Rejection was definitely a frightening possibility.

Mumbling to himself—"Cowardly wuss, Jensen Wolfe"—as he strode down the hall and away from Valynn's office (and Valynn), Jensen determined to just bide his time. Maybe he'd muster up the guts to press things a bit with Valynn one day. But for now, he'd made her smile by giving her the photos from his collection—made her happy—and that was something, after all.

It was hours before Jensen could find another excuse to drop in to Valynn's office—almost five p.m., in fact. But at least he'd found an excuse. Desirae had called to tell him that one of the frame styles Valynn had chosen for one of her gallery pieces was out of stock and not expected to be available for another two months. So as much as Jensen hated to deliver bad news, or at least frustrating news, to anyone—especially the girl he had a die-hard crush on—at least it was a pretext to talk to Valynn again.

As Jensen stepped into Valynn's office, however, he was stunned into discombobulating silence when he saw her brushing tears from her cheeks. She sniffled and dabbed at her nose with a tissue.

"Are you all right?" Jensen asked, worried at finding Valynn crying in her office.

Instantly, Valynn looked up to him, trying to force an expression of calm to her face, even as her lower lip continued to quiver.

"Yeah. Just…just a little, you know, sad," she admitted.

"About what?" Jensen immediately inquired. He was relieved to hear that Valynn wasn't injured, but the sight of the large tears rolling over her cheeks unnerved him to his core! "What's wrong?"

"Oh, nothing," Valynn said, tossing a gesture of waving something off into the air with one hand. "I'm just an emotional type of idiot."

"Why?" Jensen asked. He wanted to reach out and gather her into his arms—console her somehow. But instead, he folded his arms across his chest to keep from doing so.

"Well, after I finished up one of my other projects, I started on the photos you gave me. You know, the bridal portrait, bride and groom, and wedding party you brought in earlier."

"Yeah?" he prodded.

"Well, you know I always take them out of the folders to scan them or photograph them, of course," she began to explain. "And when I put the bridal portrait facedown on the scanner, I noticed there was writing on the back, right?"

"Yeah?" Jensen prodded again.

He felt some unseen thing pinch his heart, causing him pain, as Valynn's lower lip began to quiver again—as more tears began to spill from her eyes onto her cheek.

"She died, Jensen!" she choked in a whisper. "Only a few months after the photos were taken...only a few months after the wedding...the bride died!"

"What?" Jensen asked, frowning.

Valynn nodded, picked up the bridal portrait, which she had yet to return to its folder, and handed it to him. "See? Right there it says, *Anna (Smith) Gunderson, Married May 15th, 1921. Died July 22nd, 1921.*" Brushing the newest tears from her cheeks, she asked him, "Isn't that the saddest thing you've ever heard, Jensen? It broke my heart when I read that!"

As he read the writing on the back of the bride's portrait, Jensen felt sort of sick to his stomach. It was true—wickedly sad, but true—and he'd been the very one to hand the pictures to Valynn, to upset her so much.

"I'm so sorry, Valynn," he said, still frowning as he handed the photograph back to her. "I...I thought it would be something...something fun for you—you know, restoring these. I had no idea they were steeped in such tragedy. I'm so sorry."

But Jensen's pretty vintage photo fixer girl smiled up at him, even through her tears. "Oh, it's not your fault," she said sincerely. "They are beautiful, beautiful photographs, and I'm still in love with them. They're just sad now, and that always taints things, you know? I mean, every person in every antique photo in my own collection and yours, of course—well, every person in them has passed on. And I know that. But this was just so upsetting to read...so very sad, you know?"

She paused a moment to dab at her cute little nose with her tissue again, and Jensen selfishly hoped she'd change the subject—let him off the hook and start to recover her emotions a bit before he felt even worse about upsetting her.

But she didn't and continued, "It just makes me so melancholy, so brokenhearted, to think of the life she never got to live—the babies she never got to have and that she never got to grow old with her husband." Valynn inhaled a quiet gasping breath and explained, "But this just happens to me sometimes—an overwhelming weight of emotion, you know? Sometimes I can fend it off, but today…this one just hit me so hard."

"I feel so bad, Valynn. And I really am so sorry," Jensen said. He didn't know what else to say to try and make things better, so he awkwardly suggested, "Maybe you should take a break from working on these…or just abandon them altogether."

But Valynn shook her head. "Nope. These photographs are too beautiful to be stuffed back into storage. And besides, this beautiful, smiling bride deserves to be displayed. That way someone else, who doesn't know the tragedy of her early death, can admire her beauty, her youth, the resplendence in her smile." Valynn smiled a little, adding, "I mean, *you* know how rare it is to find professional photographs from this time period with people smiling. And I'm glad that, if she had to die young, at least her beautiful smile was preserved for her family, you know."

"Yeah…I guess," Jensen agreed—though he was still far too unsettled by Valynn's heartache to be fully aware of what he was agreeing to.

"In the past, I've figured out that it's just best to get a sad project finished, you know?" she explained to him. "Otherwise it haunts me—kind of keeps me in the depths of despair. But once it's finished, I can move beyond it, to another project, and that always cheers me right up." She looked up at him, brushing smaller tears from her cheeks, and the twinkle returned to her strikingly blue, yet still sad, eyes.

Jensen exhaled a sigh of discouragement in knowing he was responsible for her unexpected and very serious distress. "I really am so sorry, Valynn. I don't want this job to upset you like this…not ever," he offered.

But Valynn smiled at him. "Oh, don't try to act like you've never had to pretend to be happy at work when you weren't. Everybody has to at one time or another. You just caught me at a weak moment."

"What do you mean?" Jensen asked.

Valynn's smile broadened as she continued to look at him as if she were wise to his deepest secret, and Jensen could read the approval in her eyes.

"I've followed your project, you know," she began to explain. "The photographs you take for the families of terminally ill children. I saw that big magazine layout about it…the big spread you refused to be paid for." She paused, the admiration in her eyes growing, even as a few last tears trickled over her cheeks. "It's a beautiful gift to those families, you know—those happy, bright portraits you take of their loved ones who they know they're going to lose. Not to mention a real self-esteem boost to the patients." She inhaled, shook her head, and said, "I couldn't do that…at least not on the scale you do. My heart couldn't endure it. I think it would break right in two if I even attempted it."

Jensen felt his eyes narrow as he studied Valynn for a moment. She was sincere in her esteem for his project for families of terminally ill loved ones. Furthermore, he could see that she understood—she really did.

Jensen realized then that Valynn Wickley was the most empathetic person he'd ever met. Not overemotional or fragile—the terms some people used to describe those individuals who could actually feel the emotions of others. Valynn wasn't fragile at all. She was strong—strong enough to bear the burden of an empath. Jensen could see she felt for others to an even deeper depth than he did, and it awed him.

"Well, I'm still sorry the photograph upset you so badly," he said—being that he, again, couldn't think of anything else to say.

Jensen could, however, think of something to do—and before he'd really even realized his body was moving, he'd reached out and gathered Valynn into his arms, holding her against him and resting his chin on the top of her head.

"It's my fault you're crying," Jensen admitted to her. "I'm the one who handed you the project."

He exhaled a sigh of pleasure and satisfaction when he felt Valynn's arms encircle his waist in returning his embrace.

"No, I'm glad to be working on it," she said, turning her head to one side in resting it on his chest. "They're a beautiful set of photographs, and it does make me happy to know someone cares about it...about her."

Valynn tried to breathe normally—tried not to literally leap for joy and faint from elation. Heck! If she'd known Jensen Wolfe was going to wrap her in his big, strong, muscular arms and hold her against his broad, sculpted chest, she would've cried in front of him a long time before! Well, not really. Yet, being that she felt as if she'd just been pulled into Incredible Bliss Land, she knew that previously faking despair would've been worth the steamy, dreamy reward!

"Well, you can reassure me all you want," Jensen began—and Valynn loved the way she could hear the rumble of his voice resonating in his chest as he held her against him. "But I'm going to be more careful about the photographs I give to you in the future."

"Oh, no, no, no!" Valynn exclaimed, raising her head to look at him. "You have an incredible eye for beauty! I love every photo project you've given me. Yours are definitely my favorite. I feel better now. I really do," she assured him. And she did love all the photographs Jensen had given her to work on, so it worried her that maybe her emotional breakdown over the tragic bride might keep him from giving her any more.

"You feel better?" he asked as he looked down at her, sort of gazing into her eyes.

Jensen's eyes were so blue—so alluring—even when they were narrowed the way they were now as he looked at her.

"I-I really do feel better now...since you came in and I could talk about it," she confessed.

Valynn held her breath a moment as Jensen released his embrace of her body to take her face between his warm, strong hands instead. The feel of his hands on either side of her face—of their warmth, their strength held in reserve—caused so many millions of goose bumps to erupt over the surface of her body so thoroughly that, when Jensen brushed her lips lightly with one thumb, Valynn quivered with a rush of pleasure so powerful it took her breath away.

Still breathless, Valynn closed her eyes as Jensen's head descended to hers—as he pressed her lips with his in a tentative but firm kiss. His kiss was warm, incredible—and Valynn found she was able to inhale and breathe once more as Jensen kissed her a second time.

As his hands left her face, moving caressively down over her shoulders and then her arms, to settle at her waist, Valynn couldn't have fought her instincts—even if she'd wanted to, which she didn't—to wrap her arms around his neck, and she kissed him in return. No sooner had she kissed him, and simultaneously begun to wonder if the gesture were too forward for Jensen's liking, than he silently reassured her that it was very much to his liking—as he pulled her against him, pressing his mouth to hers in a more aggressive manner that coaxed Valynn into surrendering to her desire to continue kissing him.

She was sure her body was floating—that the room was spinning—that the colorful fireworks of desire flashing in her mind were, in truth, exploding in the room and not just in her imagination. Jensen Wolfe was kissing her! Jensen Wolfe! Even wrapped in the euphoria of the sensations of bliss his kiss was spreading over her, she couldn't believe it—wondered if she were dreaming.

Valynn wondered too how much practice Jensen had had at kissing women, for the way he held her, the way he kissed her, was unlike anything Valynn had ever experienced before! It was as if Jensen knew exactly how to kiss her—Valynn Wickley—in order to carry her desire higher and higher.

Yet with one final warm, moist kiss, Jensen broke the seal of their lips—gazed down at her—seemed to study her for a moment. Self-conscious shyness at realizing she'd just kissed the most handsome man in the entire world (as well as her boss) overtook Valynn then, and she dropped her arms from Jensen's neck and stepped back out of his hands.

"I'm sorry the photographs made you sad," he said.

Valynn forced a grin and shook her head—although she couldn't yet find the nerve to look up at him again. "It's…it's all part of it, you know," she stammered. She shrugged. "And I don't mind the emotions. It reassures me in a way…reminds me that I'm not heartless or unfeeling."

Finally able to look up at him again, Valynn's breath caught in her throat a moment as she was instantly reminded of how unfathomably handsome Jensen was. Still, somehow she managed another smile as she said, "And I love beautiful old photographs, no matter what the story is behind them. You know?"

Jensen nodded, grinning a little. "I do know," he agreed. He inhaled a deep breath, exhaling then and saying, "Well, I guess I'll leave you to finish it up then." He quirked one eyebrow, adding, "As long as you really are okay...and not upset with me about...anything."

Valynn smiled—a sincerely pleased smile. She wasn't sure if he were referring to the sad photographs or because he'd kissed her. Either way, she answered, "Not at all."

Jensen nodded, inhaled again, clapped his hands in front of them, rubbed them together as if he were about to embark on some demanding task, and said, "Well...I'll see you later then. Have a good evening, Valynn."

"You too," Valynn called after him as he turned and left her office.

Once Jensen was a few strides down the hall, Valynn stepped back, collapsing into her chair.

"*Ay caramba*!" she breathily exclaimed. She fanned her face in an attempt to cool her blush of sheer delight and swiveled her chair to face her desk once more.

Smiling, she picked up the photograph of the beautiful Edwardian bride who had met her end far too soon.

"Thank you!" she whispered. "See? You're still inspiring beauty, even after more than ninety years. Because let me tell you this, Anna Smith Gunderson: that kiss just now...that was the most beautiful thing I've ever experienced in my entire life!"

Uncertain as to how she would ever go back to treating Jensen as her boss and as if nothing had ever happened, Valynn carefully, gratefully, and even lovingly returned Anna Smith Gunderson's original bridal portrait to its antiquated folder.

CHAPTER SIX

The next morning, Jensen stepped into Paula's office, laying an envelope full of invoices on her desk.

"Morning," he mumbled. He was tired, being that he hadn't slept well the night before—the night following the afternoon he'd given into temptation and kissed Valynn.

"Good morning, Jensen," Paula greeted. "You look like you're still waking up this morning," she added with a wink.

"I am," Jensen admitted, yawning into one fist. "I…um…I had a lot on my mind last night, and I don't think I ever hit REM."

Paula frowned a little. "Anything I can help with?" she asked.

Jensen sighed, gritted his teeth, and considered the fact that Paula had always been a good confidant. He'd talked with her before about personal issues—several times, in fact. And although she couldn't always solve his problem, she was wiser than most people he knew and offered sound advice.

"Well," Jensen said, closing Paula's office door behind him, "I messed up…pretty badly," he confessed.

Paula's frown deepened. "How so?"

Jensen scratched his chin where his three-day whisker growth had begun to itch. "I…I…well, yesterday I gave some photos to Valynn for her to restore—you know, for gallery night."

"And?" Paula prodded.

Jensen inhaled a deep breath, exhaling it in a puff. "And later in the day when I stopped in to see how it was going, she was standing there in her office, crying!"

"Crying? Why?"

"When she was scanning one of the photos—an Edwardian bridal portrait—she saw some writing on the back, indicating that the bride had died only a few months after the wedding photo was taken. And it basically broke Valynn's heart, you know? I mean, *I* basically broke Valynn's heart."

Paula sighed with being relieved. "Oh, Jensen, for Pete's sake! Valynn's always weeping over a photo. It's who she is. She's so tenderhearted. It's not your fault the photo upset her. And I don't see how you messed up just by giving the photos to her."

Jensen exhaled a heavy breath again. "No, I messed up because…well, she was just so sad and…and so pretty…and so vulnerable…that I couldn't take it. So I kissed her."

"You what?" Paula exclaimed with pure glee.

Jensen shrugged and said, "I kissed her." He raked a hand back through his hair and added, "See? Even *you're* horrified. Imagine how Valynn feels. She has good cause to accuse me of sexual harassment at the workplace and—"

"Well, if you think she would even consider that, then you don't know Valynn as well as I thought you did," Paula interrupted.

"I know, I know. She wouldn't do that," Jensen admitted. "But I don't want her to quit either."

"Jensen," Paula began, placing a hand on his arm. She could see he was really upset, worried that he'd given Valynn cause to walk out of his life. "Did Valynn slap you when you kissed her?"

"Well…no," Jensen admitted.

Paula smiled. She felt as if she were comforting one of her own sons—helping him through some adolescent fear of rejection. It was so amusing that she might have giggled if the man hadn't looked so worried.

"Did she get mad or walk away?" Paula asked.

"No," Jensen mumbled.

"Well? What did she do?"

Jensen shrugged. "She wrapped her arms around my neck and kissed me back."

Paula smiled, patted Jensen on the shoulder, and said, "Then there you go. She obviously liked that you kissed her, so quit thinking like you're eighteen and think like the grown-up man that you are, silly boy."

"Well, the grown-up man that I am knows she has good reason to slap me with a harassment suit or quit or—" he countered.

Paula shook her head and sighed with masked frustration. "Jensen, Valynn isn't going to do that, and you know it. That's not what you're afraid of, and *I* know it. Just man up and go for it."

"Go for it?" Jensen asked. "What do you mean? Like…kiss her again?"

Paula rolled her eyes. "In the very least, idiot," she teased. She knew he was playing dumb.

"Well, I guess we'll just have to wait and see what happens," he said.

Paula recognized this behavior in Jensen as well—the let-me-squiggle-out-of-an-uncomfortable-situation act.

"Yes, I guess we will," Paula said, feigning agreement. Picking up a large folder that was lying on her desk, however, she asked, "Are you on your way to your office now?"

"Yeah," Jensen confirmed.

"Good," Paula said. Offering the large folder to him, she added, "Then you can drop this off with Valynn for me. It's a new restoration project Mr. Coleville's daughter dropped off this morning."

Jensen inhaled a deep breath, exhaling slowly as he good-humoredly glared at Paula.

"Sure thing," he grumbled. "You might as well throw me out of the frying pan and into the fire."

"Well, I guess we'll just have to wait and see what happens. Right?" Paula teased.

"I guess," Jensen said. As he turned to go, he added, "But I'm cutting you out of my will before I burn."

Paula smiled, shaking her head with amusement. How could a man that looked the way Jensen did, with such a fabulous personality and so much else to offer, be so insecure? It didn't make any sense. But, then again, Jensen's humility *was* part of his charm.

Paula sighed and returned to working on the accounting she'd been looking over. She guessed she really would just have to wait and see what happened where Jensen and Valynn were concerned. Somehow, however, she felt that the wait would be well worth it.

Jensen rubbed his whiskers a moment before stepping into Valynn's office. He felt like a fourth grader, trying to get up the nerve to talk to his crush on the playground.

Valynn was sitting at her desk with her back to her open office door. Knowing that hum-hawing around and stalling wouldn't fix anything, Jensen knocked on the doorframe and asked, "Are you busy?"

Valynn swirled around in her chair to face him. He could've sworn she was glad to see him by the way her eyes lit up as she smiled at him.

"Good morning," she cheerfully greeted.

"Good morning," Jensen greeted in return.

"What can I do for you this morning, Jensen?" Valynn asked.

Jensen couldn't help but grin as he imagined a long list of what he'd like Valynn to do for him—most of which incorporated scenarios similar to the one that had played out in her office the day before.

"A couple of things, actually," he answered instead. Stepping into her office, he offered the folder to her that Paula had sent with him. "A very supportive client had this dropped off for restoration this morning. That's thing one."

"And thing two?" Valynn asked, accepting the folder and placing it on her desk.

"Thing two is…when I came in yesterday, I forgot to tell you that Desirae says one of the frame styles you've chosen for one of your gallery pieces is out of stock and won't be available in time for gallery night."

Valynn's beautiful brows puckered together in disappointment.

"Oh, shucks," she mumbled. "What do I do now? Just go over to Desirae and see what else she has available?"

Jensen nodded. "Yep," he confirmed. "But you know Desirae. She'll probably help you find something you like even better. I mean, that's how it usually works with my stuff. I go in with one thing in mind, and Desirae flips my lid with something totally better."

"Yeah," Valynn agreed. "She's awesome. She helped me find exactly the right matte and frame styles to go with my gallery stuff." She sighed but rallied. "I'll run over and talk to her right after lunch. Thanks for letting me know."

Jensen cleared his throat, lingering uncomfortably.

"Is there anything else you need?" Valynn asked.

Again, Jensen grinned at his own mischievous thoughts.

"I, um…I wanted to apologize for yesterday," he began. He felt so awkward, and it was a strange sensation to him. He was usually pretty comfortable with other people, including women. But Valynn rattled him somehow.

"For what?" she asked.

Jensen could tell by the twinkle in her eye that she knew exactly what he was talking about. He smiled, put a little more at ease by her playing dumb.

"About…you know…kissing you," Jensen answered.

Valynn smiled. "Oh, please don't apologize for that," she giggled. "I mean, I've never been kissed by a boy as cute as you…ever!" She winked at him, her smile broadening. "It did wonders for my self-esteem. Not to mention my mood. So please don't apologize."

"But…" Jensen began. He was stunned, in truth. Could it be that she wasn't angry with him for kissing her? Not even a little bit?

"I mean, don't think I misread your intentions," she explained. "I know you were just feeling bad about being the one to give me the sad photo, even though it wasn't your fault." She laughed again. "I bet that in the history of the world there have been a lot of kisses because someone felt guilty for something, you know? But you have no reason to feel guilty, and I got to kiss the cutest boy I've ever known. So all in all, I'd call yesterday a good day, even with the sad bridal portrait. Wouldn't you?"

Jensen was still a bit stunned. Not only did Valynn seem perfectly fine with the fact he had kissed her, but she seemed to think he was attractive. Furthermore, there was something about the way she called him a cute boy that resonated inside him—made him feel flattered far beyond any compliment he'd ever before received about his appearance.

"I'm a cute boy?" Jensen couldn't help fishing.

Valynn shrugged. "Yep. The cutest!" she assured him. "I suppose my grandmother would've referred to you as a dreamboat." She tipped her head to one side, adding, "And my mom would call you a fox. But to me, you're a cute boy." She shrugged again and said, "And that's a huge compliment, believe me. If you know anything about women at all, Jensen Wolfe—beginning in about kindergarten, we all love cute boys more than anything."

Jensen couldn't help chuckling a bit. "I'll have to take you at your word then," he said. Lowering his voice, he added, "I'm not usually so forward…kissing women I work with and stuff. So thanks for trying to ease my conscience a bit."

Valynn smiled—a downright flirtatious smile—as she said, "Any time, Jensen."

Jensen's smile broadened a bit more. "I'll keep that in mind," he ventured in flirting back.

Valynn's blue eyes sparkled like starlight. Jensen didn't want to leave her company yet. He felt so good when he was around her—so hopeful and rejuvenated.

"One more thing," he began as inspiration struck.

"Yeah?" Valynn prodded.

"I have a couple coming in this afternoon to talk about their engagement photo shoot," Jensen explained. "They want an old-fashioned feel to it—you know, him dressed up in a white shirt with a celluloid collar and a vest, her in some vintage lace dress with her hair piled up. I was wondering if you'd like to sit in on the meeting with me, toss out some ideas, and, if you don't mind, assist me on the shoot in a couple of weeks."

"Me?" Valynn exclaimed. The excitement that had leapt up inside her was apparent on her face—in the rising twinkle in her eyes and her pretty smile.

"Yeah," Jensen assured her. "It sounds like a shoot you might be interested in helping me with. Plus, I figure you'll be able to help the bride-to-be with ideas for a venue, props, and such." He paused and then urged, "Are you down?"

"Oh, I'm totally down!" Valynn chirped. "I'm so excited. I can't even tell you!"

Valynn liked the way Jensen smiled at her, his gorgeous blue eyes staring right at her with obvious approval.

"All righty then," he said. "The meeting is in my office at three, okay?"

"Okay! And thank you so much, Jensen!" Valynn gushed. She couldn't help but gush. She was finally going to get to assist on a shoot—even better, one of Jensen Wolfe's personal shoots!

"Well, have a good day working on…whatever you're working on," he said. Smiling at her once more, he added, "See you at three."

"I'll be there…promptly," Valynn assured him.

"Okay," Jensen said before turning and striding out of her office.

Valynn was ecstatic! Assisting Jensen on a photo shoot? She couldn't wait! Instantly her mind began tossing ideas around. She wondered if Jensen had a venue in mind already—because, if not, she knew just the place! She wondered what the couple looked like, how exactly their clothing would appear, and what colors it would be.

Quickly, however, Valynn's thoughts bounced back to Jensen's apparent, and understandable, discomfort with what had transpired between them the day before. She was glad she'd stopped his apology cold in its tracks. After all, she'd been up all night thinking about it—relishing the wonderfulness of it—and she didn't want him ruining the experience with an apology.

Furthermore, during her restless, bliss-reliving night, Valynn had made a decision. Jensen had kissed her. And whether he meant it as merely an offering of comfort or as something else, he had kissed her—and it was an opening. If Valynn had learned one thing while working for Jensen—both from her own observations and from talking with the other employees at Wolfe, especially Paula—it was that Jensen Wolfe was not a player. He didn't collect women's hearts, or anything else a woman could offer, as trophies. He was a gentleman. And in Valynn's short twenty years of experience, she'd found that a gentleman didn't kiss a woman simply because she was crying. If nothing else, most men fled in terror when a woman was weeping. Therefore, being that Jensen had kissed her, Valynn decided to believe that there must be something about her he liked. And if there was something about her he liked, then why should she shrink away in thinking he couldn't like her even more?

Thus, as she lay in bed thinking about Jensen and about their kiss—the way it felt, so sincere and delicious—she'd determined to go for it! She wouldn't shrink away all bashful. She would flirt with Jensen, talk with him, smile at him—all sincerely, of course—and find out if there really were any possibility that the man she was in love with could somehow fall in love with her.

Naturally, she'd spent hours thinking up ways to prompt Jensen into kissing her again. Maybe she could faint in the hallway in front of him or something—pretend not to breathe and coax him into giving her mouth-to-mouth resuscitation. It was a little tricksie, but flirting and pursuing romance had always been a little that way, from the beginning of time. Valynn figured fainting would be more believable than dropping her handkerchief in his path—not that she owned a handkerchief.

Valynn also tried to think of ways she could manage to spend more time with Jensen. And that had turned into a quandary that had been bothering her all morning. And yet, lo and behold, he'd stepped into her office and asked her to assist on an upcoming shoot! Surely that would allow her to spend more time with him—at least for a little while.

All in all, Valynn was encouraged. Jensen had kissed her, and he'd come to apologize, as any true gentleman would. But she'd shown him one of her cards by asking him not to apologize and telling him he was the handsomest man she'd ever known. She smiled to herself, remembering the pleased look that had taken hold of Jensen's expression when she'd referred to him as the cutest boy she'd ever known. He'd liked it. For all the times he'd probably been told how gorgeous he was, Valynn read from his expression that Jensen liked being a cute boy. And he should like it! After all, what Valynn told him was true: girls began liking cute boys even when they were toddlers, and that never changed. After all, all handsome men were, really, were grown-up cute boys.

Knowing she had a lot of work to do, Valynn swiveled her chair back around to face her desk and computer screen. She'd have to try and focus for the next several hours—get some real work done. Maybe it would distract her from being so excited about meeting with Jensen and his clients about their photo shoot.

"Yeah right," she mumbled to herself, however. She hadn't been able to thoroughly distract herself from thinking about Jensen Wolfe since the night she first met him!

Jensen stepped into Paula's office, closing the door behind him.

Paula felt as nervous as a bunny! She knew Valynn liked Jensen and that Jensen liked Valynn. But she also knew that junk got in the way of a lot of great romances.

"Well? How'd it go?" she asked, clasping her hands together but trying to appear as calm as she could otherwise.

Jensen shrugged. "She told me not to apologize," he answered.

Paula quietly exhaled a sigh of relief. "See? I told you it was fine. Anything else?"

Jensen shrugged again as a pleased grin spread across his face. "She told me I'm the cutest boy she's ever known. I guess that's a compliment…right?"

Paula laughed then, because she knew exactly what Valynn meant. "Oh, that's an epic compliment, Jensen!" she assured him. "Women all love cute boys, from the time they're little girls. You can take that as a sign that Valynn likes you a whole lot more than she's letting on."

Jensen's smile broadened. "You think so?"

Paula nodded. "Oh, I *know* so!"

"Okay, good," Jensen sighed. "So I guess I didn't screw up too badly then."

"You didn't screw up at all, Jensen," Paula told him. She reached up, taking his whiskery face between her hands. "And let me tell you something. Go with your gut with this girl, Jensen. If your gut tells you to kiss her, then you kiss her. Got it?"

"You're telling me to pursue her?" Jensen asked.

Paula saw the worry leap to his eyes.

"Yes, I am," she confirmed. "But only if you want to, of course."

Jensen nodded. "Okay," he mumbled.

Paula dropped her hands from his face. "She's a jewel, you know."

"Yeah. I do," Jensen admitted to her. "I asked her to help me on the Firth shoot—you know, meet with them today when I do and knock around some ideas."

"Oh, that's perfect for Valynn!" Paula exclaimed. "I'm sure she'll have some incredible input."

"Yeah, I'm sure she will," Jensen agreed.

Paula smiled at him. She could tell he was nervous—uncertain of himself. But she'd said what she felt she could. Now it was time to toss him back into the pond and let him swim for himself.

"Thanks, Paula," Jensen said. "Maybe I can get some sleep tonight now."

"Heck, you're the boss," Paula reminded him. "Go catch a nap on the couch in your office for a while."

Jensen chuckled. "You're right. Maybe I will."

Jensen turned, opened the door of Paula's office, and strode away.

Paula exhaled a sigh of hope and smiled. "Good job, Valynn," she whispered to herself. "Good job."

CHAPTER SEVEN

Valynn tried to focus on the conversation at hand, but it was difficult. She was still too awed that she was sitting in with Jensen while he was discussing a photo shoot with clients!

She'd been very prompt, arriving at Jensen's office five minutes before the clients were due to be there. And when the engaged couple, Mike and Jennifer, had arrived, Jensen stood, shaking their hands and introducing Valynn even before introducing himself.

Everyone took a seat in Jensen's office, and the brainstorming began. The couple wanted a vintage look to their engagement photos, something around the turn of the last century. Valynn's mind was immediately sprinting, brimming with so many ideas that she'd stayed quiet for a few minutes as she tried to file them into some sort of order.

But when Jensen looked to her and asked, "What do you think, Valynn?"

All she could say was, "Um…a lot," in response.

Mike and Jennifer both laughed, and Jensen smiled at her with approval.

"Well, spit it out then," Jensen prodded.

The excitement was expanding so rapidly inside Valynn that she felt a little breathless as she began. "Well, first of all, if you're thinking Edwardian time period, I know the perfect place for the shoot—if you don't mind an outdoor shoot."

"Ooo! I was wanting do it outdoors!" Jennifer exclaimed with excitement. "And it's the perfect time of year for it, right, Mr. Wolfe?"

"It is," Jensen confirmed. He looked to Valynn and asked, "Is this place fairly close? And easily accessible?"

"Yes and yes," Valynn assured him. "And very private. At least most of the time, there aren't many, if any, people there—especially midday to early evening."

"What's it like?" Jennifer asked. She tucked a strand of silky blonde hair behind one ear as she leaned forward with anticipation.

"It's beautiful!" Valynn assured her. "Weeping willows, tons of beautiful grass and wildflowers." Valynn paused, leaning forward and taking Jennifer's hands in her own. "And there's a pond with beautiful grassy banks and this one place where a big willow tree is stretched out over it…and a place where we can rent you guys a vintage-looking canoe. And it will be gorgeous!"

Jennifer squealed with delight, and both Jensen and Mike laughed.

"Well, looks like we nailed the place down pretty quick," Mike said to Jensen.

"Yep," Jensen agreed, "though I would like to see it first—get some lighting readings and stuff." He looked to Valynn. "Can you take me out there this week sometime?"

Valynn's eyes widened. "O-of course," she answered. The idea of being somewhere other than work or an employee luncheon with Jensen caused a thrill to travel down her spine.

"Good," Jensen said. "So what about attire?" he asked, looking from Jennifer to Mike and back. "Do you guys already have that worked out?"

"A bit," Jennifer said. "I've got a vintage vest, shirt, and celluloid collar for Mike lined up. And"—she began digging around in her purse—"my grandma is making me this dress."

Jennifer handed the photo to Valynn, and Valynn instantly squealed with admiration. "How gorgeous! Tiered lace and everything—I love it!" she exclaimed. It truly was a beautiful gown.

Jennifer giggled. "Yeah, it's my wedding gown. I want to be legit, you know? So I'm going to wear it for the engagement photos too. But I don't know what to do about trousers for Mike."

"What color is his vest?" Valynn asked.

"Kind of a tannish taupe, you know?" Jennifer answered.

"Well then, just run to a clothing store and get him a pair of matching dress pants that don't have pleats, and you'll be fine."

"Okay," Jennifer said. "That takes a lot off my mind." Jennifer looked to Jensen then. "Mike says you guys have a hair and makeup person too? Do you think he or she could do my hair that day? I want it swept up—you know, coifed in keeping with the style of the times. But I can do my own makeup."

"You bet," Jensen said. He scribbled on a notepad he kept on his desk and then asked, "Other than a canoe, what other props, if any? I mean, we'll do the traditional types of stuff—flowers and things—but is there anything else you want?"

Mike and Jennifer looked at one another. They shrugged in unison, shook their heads, and simultaneously said, "No."

"I'd like to stick with just us and trees and grass and stuff. If that's all right with you," Jennifer said.

"Simple is best, in my opinion," Jensen commented. "We want you guys to be the focus."

"Awesome," Mike said. "So is that it?"

Jensen smiled. "Well, for now, I guess," he said. He handed them a large envelope. "Here's my estimate for the shoot, and I've included a list of print prices and copyright info. And in case you need any custom framing, there's a few suggestions there. Otherwise, I'll call you guys and let you know what time. Since Jennifer will be coming in to have her hair coifed here, you'll need to arrive early enough for that, of course. And I'll know more about travel time after Valynn and I go out there this week. Other than that, you're good to go."

Mike stood and offered a hand to Jensen. "Thanks, man," he began. "To be honest, I'm kind of ready for everything to be over."

Jensen chuckled, shook Mike's hand, and said, "It's a groom thing, I think. And very common."

Valynn was surprised when Jennifer stood up and hugged her, saying, "I'm so glad you're involved! You seem to know exactly what I'm thinking. I'm sure our photos will be beautiful!"

Valynn smiled as she returned Jennifer's hug. "Oh, they will be, but only because you guys are a beautiful couple, and you managed to snag the best photographer in the city!"

"Thank you," Jennifer giggled. Releasing Valynn, she offered a hand to Jensen. "Thank you so much, Mr. Wolfe. I'm so excited about this now!"

Smiling and shaking her hand, Jensen said, "Well, I hope you'll be happy with our results," Jensen said.

"You two have a good day," Jennifer said.

"You too," Valynn called as they left Jensen's office.

Once Mike and Jennifer were well down the hall and out of earshot, Valynn clasped her hands together and sighed, "And by the margin, willow veiled."

"What?" Jensen asked.

Valynn giggled. "The setting for Mike and Jennifer's photo shoot—it's perfectly Tennyson. You know, 'And by the margin, willow-veiled.' The banks of the place I'm going to show you are willow-veiled." When Jensen's brows puckered with not understanding, Valynn explained, "Willow trees grow near the banks of the pond, and their long branches hang over the pond. The margin in the poem refers to the banks of a river flowing down to Camelot, you know. And the margins are willow-veiled—meaning willow wands or branches hang over them, veiling them. Get it?"

Jensen nodded, arching his eyebrows with admiration. "So you're talented and well educated in literature, hmmm? Wow, my self-esteem just totally tanked out."

Valynn smiled, shaking her head. "Oh, believe me, I'm not well educated in literature. I just love poetry, and 'The Lady of Shalott' by Tennyson is one of my favorites. Actually, anyone who has ever read *Anne of Green Gables*, and thereby been lead to read 'The Lady of Shalott,' loves it. It's beautiful—just fills the mind with imagery."

"I'll have to take your word on it, being that I've never read either one," Jensen chuckled.

"Well, you don't have to have read Tennyson to appreciate this place I'm going to show you for this shoot, Jensen. It's perfect!" Valynn assured him.

And he believed her. She was, after all, as serious about her work—the quality and end result—as he was. Therefore, he had no doubt he'd find the venue she'd suggested would even exceed his expectations.

"When can you take me there?" he asked.

Valynn shrugged. "Whenever you want," she answered. "My schedule is a lot more flexible than yours, obviously. So you choose when."

Jensen pulled up his appointment calendar on his tablet. "Tomorrow?" he asked. "We could do lunch after, if you want."

Valynn exclaimed, "That would be great! Actually, we can take lunch with us, and that way you can watch the lighting for an hour or so while we eat. Does that sound good?"

It did sound good. Of course, Jensen realized it sounded a bit more like a date than a work thing—a picnic lunch under a willow tree on the banks of a pond—but if Valynn didn't seem to mind it, then he sure as hell didn't.

Valynn hoped the bags under eyes (the result of being too excited with anticipation to sleep the night before) weren't too obvious—that they didn't make her look too much like some hideous zombie. She'd taken extra care with her appearance that morning, although she chose a comfortable set of clothing, suitable for an outing to the pond that was part of Netherlander Park. Still, she'd paid detailed attention to her makeup and hair. After all, she'd be spending at least a couple of hours in the solitary company of Jensen Wolfe, so chances were he might study her appearance a little longer than normal.

As she sat in the passenger's seat of Jensen's big red pickup, she couldn't believe she was going somewhere with him! She was still astonished, of course—still wondered if she'd dreamed the kiss they'd shared a couple of days before. It seemed so surreal whenever she looked back on it—and she looked back on it a lot! Yet as they drove toward Netherlander Park, Valynn remembered their kiss very vividly—knew that it had, indeed, taken place.

"So you're telling me this place isn't a high-traffic area?" Jensen asked.

Valynn shook her head. "Not during the weekdays. It's so beautiful! But I think a lot of people like the convenience of the areas with picnic tables and fire pits, you know? It's about a half a mile walk into the park to get to this particular pond and stuff." Valynn frowned a moment as a concern reared its ugly head in her thoughts. "You don't think a half a mile walk will be a problem, do you?"

"Naw," Jensen assured her. "Besides, the park probably has a golf cart or something used for grounds maintenance. I'll check into that." He smiled and looked over to Valynn for a moment. "I mean, we certainly don't want a sweaty bride with a limp coif, now do we?"

Valynn laughed. "No, we do not!"

She stared at Jensen for a moment, just studying how incredibly cool he looked with his sunglasses on, driving his truck. He was so attractive! And it wasn't just because he was physically gorgeous. Jensen had a great sense of humor. He was nice to people—sincerely kind. He was thoughtful to his clients. Seriously, Valynn wondered how many high-end photographers would take a day to drive out to a new location on the word of the newest employee, simply because said employee had suggested it? It was because he wanted to make sure that Mike and Jennifer had the best possible engagement photos.

Of course, Valynn knew that Jensen could've taken Mike and Jennifer out to a sewage treatment plant and managed to get beautiful photographs of them. But he really wanted to please his clients, and Valynn knew the place she was thinking of would be perfect.

"So you're pretty familiar with this place, I take it," Jensen said.

Valynn nodded, sighing with gladness in the fact she was going to one of her favorite places of escape. "Yep. In fact, as gorgeous as where I'm taking you is, there's a place farther on in the park that's even more wonderful. But it's harder to get to—about another half a mile in—and it's a little more of a hike, unless you rent a canoe, which is how I usually get there. I used to go there three or four times a week when I was in high school. You know, just to be alone, shoot pictures of flowers, trees, the sky, and stuff."

"Wait a minute," Jensen said. "You rented a canoe and ventured into isolation by yourself—by canoe, I might add—when you were in high school? And your parents didn't mind?"

Valynn gulped, shrugged, and answered, "Well, you know how it is when you're a teenager—you know, how you don't always tell your parents everything you do and things?"

Jensen grinned. "Oh, I see. You forged your mom's signature on the field trip permission slip, so to speak."

Valynn giggled. "Yeah. I guess so." She paused, sighing with contentment, however. "But it's such a beautiful place, and I just wanted to go there by myself, you know?"

Jensen nodded. "I understand," he assured her. "I'm not going to rat you out to your mom."

"Gee, thanks," Valynn teased.

"I am, however, going to insist that we rent a canoe today and that you take me out to your secret, no-parents-allowed spot—once we've done recon on the place we'll be shooting Mike and Jennifer, of course," he told her.

Instantly Valynn's heart leapt inside her! She couldn't think of anything she'd rather do that day than take Jensen to her special haven and share the splendor of the day there isolated with him.

"Really?" she asked excitedly. "But don't you need to hurry back to the office?"

Jensen shook his head. "Not really," he answered. "And after all, you went to all the trouble to bring us lunch—in a picnic basket even—so why shouldn't we row out to your willow-shrouded retreat to enjoy it?"

Valynn giggled. "Willow-veiled," she playfully corrected. "And that sounds perfect! But you have to keep it a secret, okay? It would spoil it if everyone and his dog discovered it, you know."

Jensen nodded. "My lips are sealed," he assured her. "I'd tell you you could blindfold me so that I don't even know the way, but then you'd have to paddle all by yourself, and I couldn't allow that."

"How chivalrous, Jensen!" Valynn said. "And me without my parasol."

Jensen chuckled, and Valynn sighed. She knew Jensen would love the place in Netherlander Park she had in mind for Mike and Jennifer's shoot. Furthermore, if he managed to find the same sort of rest and serenity in her special haven she always had—well, add a fried chicken and potato salad picnic together, and she figured maybe Jensen would think it was just about as perfect a day as Valynn felt it promised to be.

CHAPTER EIGHT

"By the margin, willow-veiled," Jensen said, nodding. "I get it now."

Valynn smiled at him, glad he understood what she'd been talking about now that he was paddling their canoe through the water. He'd even paddled near to the pond's bank occasionally, just so the willow limbs, bursting with soft green leaves and arched out over the water's surface, could trail over his and Valynn's heads as the canoe slowly moved on.

Valynn hung one arm over the side of the canoe and let her fingertips skim over the water. "It's beautiful out here, isn't it?"

"It sure is," Jensen agreed. "The place you suggested for the photo shoot next Saturday is perfect. But it gets even better the farther in we go."

"Yep," Valynn sighed. "I love it out here."

"So this poem that you got 'willow-veiled' from," he began, prodding her to tell him more.

"'The Lady of Shalott' by Lord Alfred Tennyson," she explained. "It's a beautiful piece to read...even though it's sad."

"So by the margin, willow-veiled…I get that now. Do you know the rest of it?" he inquired.

Valynn shrugged. "I know the whole thing, but it's sad," she told him. "But you should read it, even though you're a guy. You might like it." Valynn paused a moment and then, quoting Tennyson's famous poem, recited,

By the margin, willow-veiled,
Slide the heavy barges trialed
By slow horses; and unhailed
The shallop flitteth silken-sailed
Skimming down to Camelot.

"Camelot?" Jensen asked. "Like in King Arthur's Camelot?"

"Yep, one and the same," Valynn confirmed.

"Hmm, you really are an academic, huh?" Jensen teased.

"Oh, heck no!" Valynn laughed. "I guess now that I landed the job with Wolfe Photography, I can admit that I only had a B average when I finished high school. I was way too interested in other stuff to study hard."

"Like photography and restoring old photographs?" Jensen asked with obvious understanding.

"Exactly," Valynn giggled. "I pretty much hated high school."

"I hear that," Jensen agreed. "I pretty much hated school, period. Well, after about the second grade anyway. Kids are so mean to other kids, you know? All the name-calling, bullying, and drama." Jensen shook his head. "I'm so glad I never have to go through that again. I already have anxiety thinking of my own kids going through it someday."

Suddenly, Valynn perked up. Jensen Wolfe was thinking about having kids someday? For some reason, Valynn was wildly interested in purusing that venue of conversation with Jensen.

"Me too," she said. "And I hated the stupid nicknames kids came up with for me."

"Like what?" Jensen asked, grinning at her.

Valynn rolled her eyes with exasperation at the memory. "Well, you know how kids are. It's all about the rhyming sometimes. The one I used to detest most of all was Valynn Valynn Slimy Skin. And of course there was Valynn Boleyn, Valynn Has-Been, and Valynn Violin."

Jensen offered one sarcastic, "Ha!" He shook his head, adding, "That's nothing, girl. I could only wish kids rhymed my name."

Valynn's brows furrowed with curiosity. "Well, if they didn't rhyme your name to make fun of you, what did they do?"

Jensen inhaled a deep breath, exhaling it slowly as if he were deciding whether he should answer. But at last, he offered, "They made fun of me…of my obvious physical thing that I was mortified about."

"A cute boy like you?" Valynn asked, doubtful that there was ever anything about Jensen's looks that kids could have made fun of. "What in the world could they tease *you* about?"

Jensen arched one eyebrow and asked, "So you never got made fun of for something about yourself?"

Valynn shrugged. "Well, yeah, my knobby knees," she admitted. "This one stupid fifth grader used to call me Hobbly Wobbly Dobby Knees at recess when I was in the third grade. But he called everyone something cruel like that, so no one paid him any mind really." She nodded to Jensen, exclaiming, "But you! What did you ever have to be teased about?"

Jensen smiled. "Well, thank you for the compliment and vote of confidence, but I did get teased pretty mercilessly…about my chin."

"Your chin?" Valynn asked, trying not to giggle. "What? You're kidding me! You've got, like, the greatest man-chin I've ever seen!" And it was true, after all. Jensen's chin was square and firmly set, enhanced by an ever-so-slight cleft and a jawline that looked like an artist's rendering of Adonis. How could he ever have been teased about his chin?

"Well, you just said it, in fact," Jensen told her. "You said I have a man-chin?"

"Yeah?" Valynn affirmed.

"Well, imagine having a man-chin when you're only in the fourth grade. I looked like an alien."

"You did not," Valynn said, narrowing her eyes with skepticism.

"Well, maybe not an alien," he admitted. "But I at least looked like I had that thing where your skull bones don't stop growing—I can't remember what it's called—but your head bones continue to grow your whole life. Have you ever heard of it?"

"I think so," Valynn answered.

Jensen shrugged. "Well, that's what I got teased about…my big, giant alien chin. Kids called me the Neanderthal Wolf—you know, because my last name is Wolfe and I had a huge caveman chin."

Suddenly, Valynn Violin and Valynn Has-Been didn't sound so bad. Even Hobbly Wobbly Dobby Knees seemed like less of a cut-down than Jensen's being teased about his chin by being called the Neanderthal Wolf. All at once, Valynn could imagine Jensen as a little ten-year-old boy and the pain the name would've caused him—the self-consciousness it would've washed over him.

Tears actually began to brim in her eyes as she said, "I'm so sorry, Jensen. That really was a cruel thing for kids to do…especially since it seems you were already self-conscious about it."

"I still am self-conscious about it," he said, grinning at her. "I just learned to live with it. I figure there are worse physical deformities people are born with and have to endure. So mine isn't bad in comparison."

"Physical deformities?" Valynn exclaimed, sitting upright in the canoe and causing it to rock a little too strongly. "You have a beautiful chin! It's perfect for you! Most men can only wish for a chin like yours." Valynn's eyes narrowed as she said, "In fact, since I met you, there have been many times that I've thought of what a good photography subject you would be. I mean, I could take a beefcake picture of you that would spin any woman's head off, you know?"

Jensen laughed—really laughed with sincere amusement. "Oh, you kill me sometimes, Valynn," he said through his laughter. "The stuff you come up with, I swear."

"But I mean it," Valynn assured him. "The very day I first saw you—or rather that first evening I saw you—I thought of what a good subject you would be. I wondered why I'd never seen a photograph of Jensen Wolfe anywhere before. I mean, you really keep under the radar, you know? And I thought, I could shoot that guy in a way that would make old ladies' heads spin right off their necks! That's really what I thought."

Jensen laughed again. "Oh, did you now?"

"Yes," Valynn said. "And I still can't believe you got teased about your chin. How mean."

Jensen's brows arched in disbelief as he saw Valynn brush a tear from each eye. She was crying? She felt so bad about what he'd endured as a child that she was crying for him? He opted to behave like he didn't notice her tears, but the fact she felt so tenderly toward the boy he'd once been made him feel warm inside.

"A beefcake photo, huh?" he chuckled. "Well, in case you haven't figured it out, I don't like to have my picture taken."

"Why not? I mean, I don't like to have mine taken either. But you…that doesn't make sense because I can tell you're very photogenic," she told him.

"Is that so?" he asked. She was so funny, the way she spoke to him like she'd known him her whole life.

Jensen was very glad Valynn had thought of Netherlander Park for Mike and Jennifer's shoot—and because it was a good photo-op spot was the least of the reasons he was glad.

As he slowly paddled the canoe, he studied her a moment—the way the sun made her hair look lighter and seemed to bring out the pink in her cheeks—the way she was sitting so comfortably in the canoe, letting her small fingers trail over the water's surface now and then. The fact was, Valynn Wickley was just too cute, too pretty, too beautiful on the inside and the outside for her own good. Jensen was hoping that the place she was leading him to now was as secluded as she claimed it was, for he'd decided to take Paula's advice: just man up and go for it.

After all, why shouldn't he make a play at winning Valynn's attention—her heart? He was more attracted to her, more entertained by her, and just overall more pleased with her company than he'd been with any other woman he'd ever known. So why not see if she could feel more for him than just thinking he was a cute boy?

"Oh wait! We're here!" Valynn exclaimed, sitting upright in the canoe again. "I almost missed our stop. Pull in right here...under this big willow here."

Jensen smiled, glad they'd reached their destination. For one thing, he was starving. But most of all, he wanted to spend time alone with Valynn. Any woman that would defend his caveman chin the way Valynn had—well, he was more and more dazzled by her.

"Thank you," Valynn said as Jensen helped her to step out of the canoe. "I feel like I should add 'kind sir' to that," she giggled. After all, it was an entirely dreamy, entirely vintage situation—being paddled in a canoe across a duck-spotted pond to a secluded grassy hideaway, a haven covered with lush grasses warmed by the sun, enormous willow trees to provide cooling shade—two of which had a tattered cord hammock tied between them— fluffy white clouds drifting overhead in a brilliant blue sky, and, best of all, no one else even close to being nearby!

"How come I never knew Netherlander Park had these kinds of nooks and crannies, hmm?" Jensen asked as he tugged the canoe completely to shore. Lifting the picnic basket out of the canoe, he added. "Seriously, I've done a million shoots in Netherlander, and I never knew all this was back here."

"But you see," Valynn began, "that's exactly the point. It's not as public as the rest of the park. That's part of its charm. A person has to really know it's here, or at least go looking for it, to find it. That's one reason I love it so much."

Jensen nodded as he glanced around at the scenery. "It's great out here. I can see why you used to sneak away to get here." He looked at her then, smiled, and said, "But I'm starving, so can we eat first and enjoy serenity later?"

Valynn laughed. "Of course! I'm hungry too. I was too nervous to eat breakfast this morning."

"Why?" Jensen asked unexpectedly.

His question caught Valynn off-guard, and she wasn't sure how to answer. She certainly couldn't tell him she'd been nervous that morning because of the near frantic anticipation she'd experienced at knowing she was going to spend part of the day alone in his company.

Therefore, she rallied with, "I…I was worried you wouldn't like the place I'd thought of for Mike and Jennifer's shoot."

"Well, you didn't have any reason to doubt it because you were right. It's perfect," he reassured her.

Valynn smiled, her heart swelling with pride in having pleased Jensen. "Well, I'm so glad you liked it. And I can just imagine what you can shoot there." Pointing to a nearby willow tree, she said, "Let's have lunch right over there, under that tree."

"Looks good," Jensen agreed.

They walked together to the tree, ducking under the willow's long branches as they reached it.

Jensen set the picnic basket down on the grass, and Valynn opened it, pulling out the thin red-and-white–checked blanket she'd brought.

"Wow!" Jensen said, smiling as he watched her spread the picnic cloth over the grass. "You don't mess around with picnics. I don't know if I've ever seen a picnic blanket that actually looked just like someone snatched it out of an old '50s movie like that."

Valynn giggled. "Sometimes I'm a stickler for details, and sometimes I'm not. But this picnic blanket…it's one of my stickler details." Patting a place on the picnic blanket, she said, "Okay, now sit down right here, and I'll get the food ready."

"Ahhh," Jensen sighed as he first sat down on the picnic blanket and then stretched out on his side.

"I love fried chicken for picnics," Valynn explained as she lifted a large plastic container out of the basket. "And potato salad, of course," she added as she withdrew a smaller container.

Jensen smiled, delighted by her domesticity. He figured that if she were wearing a skirt, sweater, and string of pearls around her neck, instead of her shorts and pink top, she'd look like she stepped right out of some 1950s television show.

"Here," she said, handing him a plastic tumbler with a lid, filled with what looked to be lemonade. "Lemonade for you and water for me," she added, lifting another tumbler from the basket.

"Why do I get the lemonade?" Jensen asked.

"Because I hate it," Valynn answered, smiling at him. "But since I'm the only person I've ever known that hates lemonade, I took a chance that you might like it. I do have an extra water if you'd rather have that though."

"No, I like lemonade," Jensen assured her. He arched one eyebrow with curiosity. "Although I will admit that I've never met anyone who didn't like lemonade before."

Valynn shrugged. "Yeah. Most people do."

"Why don't you like it?" he asked.

Valynn continued to pull items out of the picnic basket—napkins, plastic plates, plastic spoons—and Jensen loved watching her every move.

"Well, to be honest," she began, "when I was about seven, my family took a little trip to the mountains. We brought along a picnic lunch—fried chicken, potato salad, the works!"

Jensen smiled, amused by the way her eyes sparkled as she reminisced.

"Including a big glass jug of lemonade," Valynn added. She sighed, sitting back on her heels and gazing up into the tree branches a moment. "I can still remember it—the way the big jug of delicious-looking lemonade was sitting there on a tree stump, sparkling in the sun."

"So I take it you used to actually like lemonade?" Jensen urged.

"Yep! Loved it," Valynn admitted. "Until a few minutes after we'd set out everything for the picnic."

"What happened?"

Valynn looked at Jensen, grimacing with disgust. "My baby sister went number two in her diaper, and it was so soft and messy that it started oozing out everywhere."

Jensen chuckled. "And it ruined your appetite, I take it."

"No. Not really. But my parents had forgotten to bring any water with us," Valynn explained. She shrugged. "So my dad and mom used the lemonade to wash her up…and then guess who got to hold the very sticky baby all the way home? The very sticky baby who reeked of baby poo blended with lemonade. Me!"

Jensen couldn't keep from chuckling. And as he laughed, Valynn did too, and it was further proof of her great sense of humor—the fact she could laugh at herself.

"It was sickening!" she continued. "I almost threw up several times on the way home, and it was an hour-long drive, by the way. Then, after that, I never liked lemonade ever again."

"Well, I have to admit, that would pretty much scar a kid for life," Jensen offered.

"Yeah, it did," Valynn affirmed. She giggled a little then and said, "The funny thing is that my little sister loves lemonade! Ha ha ha! To this day, she'll choose lemonade over any other drink if she has the chance, even over milk or water." Valynn shook her head, still amused by the memory. "I mean, you already know I have issues with feces—flyspecks and stuff—and now you know that contributes to the reason I don't like lemonade too."

Jensen couldn't contain himself any longer. As he began to laugh more boldly, he said, "You have issues with feces? You're hilarious, Valynn."

"But I do," Valynn assured him—although she too joined in a more hearty form of laughter.

Still laughing, Jensen offered, "Well, I think most people do."

"Well, yeah, except maybe scatologists," Valynn said.

"What-ists?" he asked.

"Scatologists. You know, people that study feces," she explained.

Jensen was laughing again but managed to ask, "You're telling me that you know what people who study manure are called?"

Valynn nodded. "Sure. I look stuff up like that. And though I'm not really a coprophobic—because I don't *fear* feces necessarily—I do have issues with it. So one day I was wondering if there were people who actually found it interesting, and there are. They're called scatologists or coprologists."

Jensen wiped the moisture of intense amusement from his eyes as he sighed in finishing up his laughter. "Well, Valynn, I have to say that I've already learned more about you in five minutes than I know about most people I've known for years."

"That's a good thing, right?" Valynn ventured.

Valynn liked that she'd managed to entertain Jensen—inadvertent though it may have been. Finding humor in everyday life was important. It helped make the more dramatic times easier to weather.

"It's absolutely a good thing," Jensen agreed. "I just think it's kind of…kind of unexpected."

Jensen smiled at her, and Valynn's heart leapt with excitement and hope.

"Golly, I hope I didn't spoil your appetite with telling you my lemonade and baby poo story," she commented.

"Not at all," Jensen assured her. "I just hope I didn't offend you by laughing."

Valynn giggled. "Naw. I think it's funny too. You see," she continued as she spooned some potato salad out onto a plastic plate for him, "I didn't put that together all at once," she explained. "It wasn't until…oh, a year or two ago when someone asked me if I wanted some lemonade at a party that I suddenly connected the dots as to the birth of my disdain toward lemonade. And when I figured it out, I thought it was funny too. Even though it didn't help me like lemonade any better."

"Yeah, I suppose we all have strange stuff like that," Jensen noted.

Valynn took the lid off the chicken container and held the container toward him.

As he selected a drumstick, he continued, "It's either baby poop and lemonade or having a Neanderthal chin in elementary school. One way or the other, everyone has issues." He paused a moment and then added, "I mean, you know how it is being a photographer. Rarely do I have a client who doesn't have some sort of hang-up about their appearance. In their minds, either their nose is too big or their smile is too gummy…and all because someone probably made fun of them when they were a kid." He looked up, grinned at her, and said, "Or their baby sister had a messy diaper and got washed up with lemonade once, and you don't dare offer them a glass of lemonade as a courtesy, you know?"

"I *do* know," Valynn laughed. She sighed then, however, looked at Jensen, and said, "You really do have a great chin though. You know that now, right?"

Jensen sat up and took a swig of lemonade from his tumbler. "Well, if you say so," he rather mumbled. "But I still see the Neanderthal Wolf when I look in the mirror every morning."

"Well, you shouldn't," she playfully scolded.

Jensen shrugged and then asked, "So you don't feel self-conscious anymore about your knees because kids teased you?"

All at once, Valynn did feel a bit more self-conscious about her knobby knees. She was wearing shorts and sitting pretzel style.

"Well, only when cute boys mention them," she teased.

Jensen chuckled, shook his head, and said, "Well, if my opinion means anything to you…I think your knees are downright sexy."

"Okay, now you're just being a dork," she giggled.

"Nope," he said, taking another swig of lemonade. "I checked them out quite thoroughly—earlier when you didn't know I was looking—and I'd say you've got the best pair of knees I've ever seen."

"Oh, you're just trying to make me feel better because I like your chin," Valynn laughed.

But Jensen shook his head as he took a bite of his chicken leg. "Nope," he mumbled as he chewed. "I keep trying to think of a reason to touch them."

Valynn burst into laughter. "Okay! Now you're being ridiculous!"

"How do you know?" Jensen teased, trying to maintain a frown of being serious. "Maybe I have a thing for knees."

"Oh, you do not," Valynn squealed with delight at his flirting.

"Which reminds me," Jensen began. He nodded toward the old hammock stretched between the tree they were sitting under and the one closest to it. "Have you ever given that old hammock a try?"

"My knees remind you of that hammock?" Valynn giggled.

Jensen smiled. "No. But I was just wondering if you'd ever been in that hammock. I know hammocks were a big deal way back when. You see a lot of vintage postcards and snapshots with people posing in hammocks."

"Yeah," Valynn agreed. "*Awkwardly* posing in hammocks. I mean, really, have you ever seen a good photograph of anyone in a hammock?"

"Come to think of it, no," Jensen admitted.

Valynn was surprised when Jensen laid his chicken leg back on his plastic plate, stood up, and offered her his hand, saying, "Come on. Let's try it out. Wouldn't it be cool if we could rig up a hammock for Mike and Jennifer's shoot?"

"It will never work," Valynn assured him—although she took his hand and allowed him to help her up all the same. "It's too awkward," she said, "unless you maybe arranged them in it the other way—you know, crosswise of the way the hammock is tied. Hammocks made out of cording like this one stretch out pretty far side to side, I think."

Valynn was elated, bliss-filled by the fact that Jensen held her hand as they walked the short distance to the hammock. The beauty of the day seemed to erupt into even more glory as Jensen stretched out in the hammock, motioning for her to join him.

"Come on, Valynn," he coaxed with an alluring smile. "Let's see if we can make this work for the engagement shoot."

Valynn put her hands on her hips and shook her head. "It won't work. It's difficult enough for one person to pose in a hammock and make it look truly comfortable, let alone two."

Still, the truth was, she wanted nothing more than to crawl into the hammock with Jensen. For one thing, if they really could figure out how to make it work—how to disguise the awkward positions that occurred when two people were in a hammock together—it really could be a wonderful possibility for Mike and Jennifer's photo shoot. But most of all, Valynn simply wanted to cuddle with Jensen in the hammock—be close to him again, held in his arms again, even if it were for only a few seconds.

"We can do it," Jensen encouraged her, however. "We'll have to be careful with Jennifer's dress, of course. But we can make it work. Come on." He paused a moment and then grinned with mischief. "What's the matter? You chicken?" he teased.

Remembering the conversation she'd witnessed between Paula and Jensen concerning the old movie *Back to the Future*, Valynn countered, "Who do you think I am? Marty McFly?"

"Ooo, the girl knows her movies," Jensen teased. His eyes narrowed as he stared at her for a few moments. "So?" he asked. "Are you chicken? Or do you want to try and make Mike and Jennifer's photo shoot really perfect for them?"

"Fine!" Valynn giggled. Then, wagging an index finger at Jensen, she added, "But no touching my knees, you knee-obsessed weirdo. And I still don't think it will work."

"Come on in, the water's fine," Jensen chuckled as he attempted to stretch the excess cording of the hammock out at his side.

"I'm telling you, this is not going to work," Valynn laughed as she very awkwardly climbed into the hammock with Jensen.

No sooner had Valynn managed to completely get into the hammock, however, than she found that the cording of the hammock did exactly what she had expected it to do: it tightened, curled, and wrapped her and Jensen so tightly into its clutches that she could hardly move.

Valynn laughed as Jensen began to chuckle as well.

"You see?" she giggled. "I told you! It's like getting your fingers out of one of those paper Chinese handcuff things! There's no way this will make a good photo op. I told you this wouldn't work."

Jensen's chuckling stopped rather abruptly, however, and as Valynn lay face-to-face with him, gazing into his mesmerizing blue eyes, he said, "Who said it didn't work?"

"What?" Valynn asked.

Jensen grinned, reached out, and brushed a strand of hair from Valynn's cheek. The gesture caused a powerful thrill to travel over Valynn's entire body.

"How dumb do you think I am?" he asked in a lowered voice.

As Jensen's gaze lingered on her mouth—as goose bumps of anticipation rippled over her arms, her legs, and even her knobby knees—Valynn realized she'd been caught, captured in the hammock by a wily hunter.

"Obviously not as gullible as I am," she answered, smiling at him. "You already knew this would never present a good photo opportunity."

Jensen smiled at her, caressing her cheek with the back of his hand. "Well, that doesn't mean I didn't know it would present an even better opportunity."

Valynn bit her lip with pure, untainted pleasure. Jensen meant to kiss her again! She could see it in his eyes—feel it in the way his thumb rested on her lips a moment.

All at once, and seemingly out of nowhere, a quintet of tiny, iridescent hummingbirds appeared, hovering for several long seconds just above the hammock. The sound of their fragile wings rapidly fluttering overhead was soothing to Valynn. And even though the tiny visitors flew away almost as quickly as they had arrived, Valynn knew that hummingbirds were said to be a sign of, among other things, courage, joy, loyalty, and affection.

Therefore, when she looked back to Jensen—as his eyes narrowed as he grinned at her—Valynn decided to pretend that the beautiful little birds had arrived to give her a tiny token of confidence, a belief that maybe Jensen Wolfe really liked her as much as it was beginning to appear he did.

CHAPTER NINE

"You picked the perfect place for the engagement shoot, Valynn," Jensen mumbled in a low, provocative voice. "Not to mention the perfect place for this."

Jensen kissed Valynn once—a firm but somewhat tentative kiss. Then, grinning at her, he said, "And I'm not going to try and apologize this time."

Valynn smiled. "Oh, please don't," she whispered.

And then, Jensen kissed her again—lightly kissed her upper lip, teasingly kissed her lower lip—before finally pressing his mouth to hers in a tender kiss that sent butterflies startling to flight in her stomach and a pleasurable shiver racing down her spine.

His kiss was warm, soft, and tinged with something—some sort of velvet voodoo that made her lips tingle with pure delectation! Slowly his mouth began to coax her lips to parting, and as the warm tenderness of his kiss gave way to fervid, moist demand, Valynn's heart swelled so powerfully inside her that she was momentarily breathless. Valynn briefly thought of one of her favorite moments in childhood fiction: the moment when Dr. Seuss's Grinch experiences his heart growing two sizes—thought that her own heart had just done the same. And as Jensen continued to kiss her—as she continued to kiss him in return—Valynn wished she could linger there forever—linger with a dreamboat in a hammock—linger in kissing Jensen Wolfe, the man who had unconsciously captured her heart.

Jensen was lost—lost to his desire to kiss Valynn—lost to his admiration of her, his affection for her, his increasing and eager yearning to win her and keep her for his own. She was so beautiful, so kind and sweet, so empathetic, and she made him laugh—made him happy. Wrapping her tightly in his arms—even for the fact that the hammock's cording and the weight of their bodies against it had done most of the work of embracing for him—Jensen kissed her hard, drawing encouragement from her responses to him. Valynn's mouth was so warm and somehow desperate for Jensen's. Therefore, he didn't pause in attempting to indulge her obvious enjoyment of their passionate exchange.

Jensen wanted Valynn for his own; in that moment, he was entirely sure and willing to do whatever he had to do to win her. Swept away by emotion, desire, and determination, Jensen unconsciously shifted his weight in the hammock. Unexpectedly, the hammock began to twist. And before he'd even really realized what was happening, Valynn tumbled out of the hammock, and he followed her, as the uncooperative tangle of cording spilled them out onto the grass.

At once, Valynn began to laugh. And though Jensen was miserable with disappointment that their romantic interlude had ended, her adorable laughter not only was contagious but also eased the awkwardness of the moment.

Rolling from lying on top of Valynn where the hammock had deposited him and onto his back, Jensen laughed with her.

"Well, you were right," he said. "There ain't no way to take a good photograph of two people lying in a hammock."

"I told you!" Valynn managed as she continued to laugh.

Jensen rolled over, gathering Valynn in his arms. "But it sure is conducive to trapping a pretty girl and forcing her to let you kiss her."

He smiled, feeling happy and contented as Valynn returned his embrace, wrapping her arms around his neck and saying, "Oh, you don't have to trap me in order to kiss me, you know."

"I don't?" Jensen asked, taking the awesome bait.

"Nope," Valynn teased.

Jensen's eyes widened when she suddenly wrapped her legs tightly around his, said, "But you might want to hold on," and somehow managed to start them both rolling down the grassy hill that the hammock had poised them atop when it had spilled them out.

Putting one hand at the back of Valynn's head to protect her from any harm or injury, Jensen smiled as he was able to propel their tumbling to a much greater velocity by using his superior weight and physical strength.

It was nothing if not a rather bumpy trip to the foot of the hill, but Jensen adored the way Valynn giggled all the way down.

Landing in a heap at the bottom of the hill, Valynn felt Jensen let go of her and roll over on his back. Valynn laughed and laughed as she too lay on her back, staring up at the sky and noting how her dizziness made the fluffy white clouds look like a spinning mobile over a baby's crib.

The grass was cool and refreshing beneath her, and the sound of Jensen chuckling with residual amusement made her happy.

Panting a bit, she offered, "Wow! I'm obviously not as young as I once was. That one roll-down made me dizzy!"

"That's because you went at it like a Kamikaze," Jensen laughed. "I haven't done that in probably fifteen or twenty years! I feel like I've been thrown into a vertigo spasm or something."

Valynn laughed, even as she continued to try and catch her breath and let her equilibrium reset.

"So? What do you think?" she asked Jensen.

"About what?" he countered. "About the place for the photo shoot? The fact that we left our lunch up at the top of the hill—in more ways than one, I'm afraid—or what?"

Valynn rolled over on her side, propped her head on one hand, and explained, "About letting me do a beefcake photo of you as one of my gallery night pieces."

Jensen burst into laughter. "Oh, yeah right!" he exclaimed. "That's what I want more than anything in the world—a bunch of clients as well as complete strangers thinking I'm a cocky son of…a cocky, narcissistic, closet nudest."

"Oh, come on," Valynn urged. "I can do a very cool, very tasteful shot and even leave most of your face out of it, if you like. Although…your face is my favorite thing about you."

Jensen rolled onto his side so he faced her. Propping up an elbow, he braced his head on his hand. "Okay…what do you want? A raise?" he asked, smiling at her.

"No, of course not," Valynn said, rolling her eyes. "I just want to have a great picture of you that exists somewhere in the world…and in my personal collection."

"Mmm, I don't really go in for photographs of myself," Jensen mumbled.

"But you understand what I mean, don't you?" Valynn began. "You would be so easy to shoot, and I would love to try and do a great, fun photo of you. I'm a true believer that every man should have a beefcake-ish photo of himself and that every woman should have a glamour photo of herself, taken while they're still in their prime. You know, so that they can show their children and grandchildren what they looked like before."

Jensen studied Valynn's expression for a moment. He could tell she was sincere, but he was more than just excruciatingly uncomfortable with her proposition.

He grinned with amusement and with being flattered, however, when she continued to attempt to convince him. "I mean, I have this one snapshot of my grandpa when he was in the navy, you know. He was on his ship's deck, wearing pants but no shirt, and he was young and vibrant and smiling and looked so handsome! It was my grandmother's favorite picture of him, and she still keeps it stuck to the front of her refrigerator with a magnet. I got her to let me scan it and do a little restoration, and I had a copy framed for my mom's house. It's awesome! That's all I'm talking about, Jensen—not some Channing Tatum movie still for those male stripper movies he does."

Jensen couldn't help but laugh out loud again. The comparisons Valynn made were so funny!

Jensen inhaled a deep breath, exhaling slowly and wishing his head would finally quit spinning. He wanted nothing more in that moment than to please the woman he had become infatuated with, so he said, "I'll tell you what. I'll let you do some stupid beefcake photo of me, if you let me shoot a portrait of you."

But Valynn shook her head emphatically. "Now wait, that's not the same, and I'm not like you. I don't—"

"Come on, Valynn. Fair is fair," Jensen reminded her. "We could do it on the same day—at the offices on a Saturday when no one else is around."

Valynn frowned at him a little but asked, "What kind of portrait?"

"How about head-and-shoulder shots, vintage look—like '40s or '50s," he explained. "You know, like the old black-and-white glamour setups back then."

"Okay, I'll admit that *that* intrigues me," Valynn said, smiling.

"I figured it would," Jensen chuckled. "So how about it? We meet at the studio on Saturday at, say, ten a.m. and do some experimenting with each other?"

Valynn gasped, giggled, and said, "Well, that sounds terrible!"

Jensen laughed and said, "You know what I mean. So what do you say?"

Valynn sighed, staring at him for a long time in a way that made Jensen's stomach start twisting into knots with desire and longing.

"Okay," she said at last. "Saturday morning at ten a.m. But let's do mine first, because I'll have my hair and makeup done to fit the style you're planning to shoot."

"Done," Jensen agreed.

"You drive a hard bargain, Mr. Wolfe," she said as she rose to her feet and offered him her hand to help him up. "But I really do want to shoot you badly enough to agree to it."

Taking her hand and pulling himself to his feet, Jensen said, "It would seem so. Now how about we get back up there to our lunch? I'm still starving. And your little rolling-down-the-hill antics made me even hungrier. I think we jacked my stomach up or something."

"Sorry," Valynn giggled. "Still, you deserved it for luring me into that hammock with you."

"Yeah, I guess I do," Jensen admitted, smiling.

"I mean, you could've just told me your plan, you know?" Valynn flirted.

Again Jensen's stomach twisted with wanting to take Valynn in his arms and enjoy a repeat of their time together in the hammock.

"Is that so?" he flirted in return.

"Yep," Valynn assured him as she started walking back up the hill toward the willow tree that hovered over their picnic.

Jensen followed her up the hill, studying her from behind the whole time. The girl was gorgeous—back to front, front to back, and head to toe. In fact, Jensen was so distracted by watching Valynn, he didn't see the large bird suddenly fly out of the willow tree as they reached the top of the hill.

"Look out!" Valynn squealed as she saw a bird flitter out of the willow tree just as she and Jensen reached the top of the hill once more.

But she had warned him too late and covered her mouth as she gasped when the bird let go right over Jensen.

"Sick!" Jensen exclaimed as he looked to see bird manure all over one shoulder. "Freaking birds," he grumbled. "I swear they do it on purpose, you know?"

"I know," Valynn agreed.

She watched then, awed with admiration, as Jensen did not pause a moment in stripping off the black T-shirt he'd been wearing. Wadding the shirt up, he dabbed at his shoulder in case any of the bird manure had managed to soak through to his skin. Valynn was dazzled—awestruck by the perfect male physique standing before her. Old Channing Tatum had nothing on Jensen Wolfe where perfectly sculpted torso, stomach, and abdominal muscles were concerned! She knew Jensen was movie-star handsome—knew he was muscular from the way his shirts fit and the way it felt to be in his arms. But she had no idea just how faultlessly beefcakey he actually was!

"Yep," she muttered to herself. "Give me my camera, and, oh yeah, I can work with that!"

"What?" Jensen asked, still wiping at his shoulder.

"Um…I…um," Valynn stammered.

He looked over to her then, grinned, and asked, "Were you getting ready to offer me some of that lemonade you brought?"

Trying to will away the blush that had risen to her cheeks, Valynn answered, "Har har. Remember, experience has taught me to bring along water too. Let's get you washed off a bit, just in case that bird feces soaked through."

"Oh, that's right," Jensen said. Grinning with recognizable mischief in mind, he tossed his T-shirt to the ground. "You have issues with feces," he said as he reached out, gathered her into the powerful vise his arms provided, and took her down in the grass.

Valynn squealed as, once more protecting her head with one hand, Jensen sent them on a second tumble down the hill together.

This time when they reached the bottom of the hill, however, Jensen didn't release Valynn. Instead, as she lay beneath him trying to catch her breath, he smiled, brushed her hair from her face, and kissed her squarely on the mouth.

"You make me laugh, Valynn," he mumbled against her lips.

"Well, you give me butterflies in my stomach," she whispered.

As Jensen kissed her again—as his mouth blended with hers in a sort of kiss that made her body feel weak, numb even—Valynn slid her arms around his shoulders, running her hands up over his neck to weave her fingers through his hair. She didn't care that there might still be bird manure residue on one broad, smooth shoulder. She just wanted to kiss him and be kissed by him. When he kissed her, it seemed like anything were possible—like every one of her secret dreams of what she wanted in life were possible.

All too soon, Jensen broke the seal of their mouths, stood, and helped Valynn to stand as well.

"Come on, lemonade girl," Jensen said as he took Valynn's hand and began leading her back up the hill. "I better eat before you have to have me life-flighted out of here because of malnutrition."

Valynn laughed. "Is that all boys think about? Food?"

Jensen smiled and answered, "Food and tricking pretty girls into getting into hammocks with them, yeah."

Valynn smiled, her heart bursting with happiness. He thought she was pretty! He'd flat out said it! Well, in so many words he'd said it—in a round-about way he'd said it. Valynn was elated because now that she knew for sure that Jensen thought she was attractive—now that she knew for sure he had coaxed her into the hammock just so he could be close to her—well, she felt like the ball toward perhaps winning his heart entirely for her own was rolling.

And as they sat on her red-and-white–checkered picnic blanket, under her favorite willow tree, eating fried chicken and potato salad and engaged in entertaining conversation, Valynn's daydreams of how wonderful life could be if Jensen Wolfe were her own soared to meet the velvet white clouds that floated overhead in that marvelous sky of blue.

CHAPTER TEN

"It's kind of crazy," Jensen mumbled as he looked through his camera viewfinder at the beautiful young woman he was photographing. "It's like a window to the past, you know?"

"Well, I hope so," Valynn giggled. "It took me an hour and a half to get to this point. That's why I needed to go first."

If Jensen didn't know better, he would've thought some angel who had once lived in a bygone era had walked into his studio.

Valynn's attention to detail floored him! When she walked in all dolled up in perfect 1940s fashion—complete with her hair in Betty Grable victory rolls on top and loosely hanging in a net snood in back—Jensen's jaw had nearly dropped to the floor.

She was wearing a black, form-fitting dress that boasted the shoulder-pad style of the era, black ankle-strapped heels, and stockings with seams up the back of her calves and thighs. Her makeup was also perfectly in fitting with the glamorous, silver-screen look of the World War II years, as well. In fact, her flawlessly applied red lipstick was distracting in its invitation to be kissed.

As Jensen pressed his camera shutter button over and over again, he found that he literally salivated every once in a while over how beautiful Valynn was—and how easy she was to shoot. And Valynn knew just how to pose, like she was born to it.

All too quickly, Jensen set his camera down. Shaking his head, he said, "Well, I have to say it, Valynn. I've never had an easier time shooting anyone…not ever."

"That's because I take pictures too, so I know the angles you need," Valynn reminded him. Clapping her hands together with excitement, she hurried over to him then. "And now…now it's my turn!" she squealed with happiness.

Jensen exhaled a heavy sigh of discouragement. "You're really going to make me go through with this?" he asked.

He didn't want to be photographed. All he wanted to do was whisk Valynn up in his arms and kiss the lipstick right off her mouth!

"A deal is a deal," Valynn reminded him.

Jensen hung his head a moment, and she laughed. "Oh, what are you complaining about? You just had to roll out of bed, throw on some clothes, and show up. I had to primp for an hour and a half!"

"Hey," he teasingly scolded, "I'll have you know I spent my time getting ready this morning. I bet it took me a whole half an hour to get showered, dressed, and stuff."

Valynn laughed. "Oh, the torture," she mocked. She sat down on a chair and began to unbuckle an ankle strap of one shoe.

"No, no, no. Leave the outfit just as it is," Jensen said. He smiled, winked at her, and added, "It will help to motivate me to go through with this." He took one of Valynn's hands in his, raised it to his lips, and kissed the back of it. "You look…well, downright seductive."

"Okay, now you're just trying to squiggle out of letting me shoot you," Valynn said. "But it's not going to work. Go stand over there in front of the backdrop. I'll try to make this as quick and as painless as possible."

Dropping her hand and letting his shoulders sag with discouragement, Jensen did what she told him. "All right, what do you want me to do now?" he asked.

"That's a very loaded question, Mr. Wolfe," Valynn teased as she removed her camera from its case.

When she again looked up at Jensen, the perfect specimen of masculinity that he was, she held her breath in awe a moment. Head to toe he was so attractive, and she felt excess moisture flood her mouth as she thought of his kiss.

"I promise that this won't take long at all," Valynn told him. "We'll start with just a head shot or two—you know, to help you relax."

But Jensen chuckled. "I can guarantee you that I won't relax at all until this is over."

"Oh, come on," Valynn said, shooting a couple of shots of Jensen as he nervously ran his fingers back through his hair. "You know better than anyone that the sooner you cooperate with me, the faster the torture will be over."

"Yeah, yeah, yeah," Jensen grumbled.

Valynn watched through her viewfinder as Jensen inhaled a deep breath, gritted his teeth to set his jaw squarely, and began posing stances that were perfect for what Valynn wanted.

"See? I knew it! You've done this before!" she exclaimed as her shutter clicked rapidly.

"No, I've shot this before," Jensen chuckled. "And I know what I would be telling me to do. And here's your warning: you have three more minutes, and then I can't take this any more, okay?"

"Agreed," Valynn said. She knew he was uncomfortable—that no matter how perfectly beefcakey he was or how he was posed, he was miserable. Therefore, she shot him in action mode so that she would have as many options as possible for her gallery piece.

"Okay, a minute and a half," Jensen called out.

Valynn smiled, giggling as she watched him strip off his shirt and flex seemingly every muscle in his body while still managing to look as if he were relaxed, careless, and casual.

"Thirty seconds," Jensen said.

"I know! I know!" Valynn exclaimed. "Now stop. You're making me nervous."

"Well, you've been making me nervous since you walked in that door this morning," Jensen said.

Through the viewfinder, Valynn watched Jensen as he began to stride toward her—her shutter clicking away—until all at once, she realized he wasn't posing any longer.

"Here," Jensen said as he reached her. "Put that down."

He took Valynn's camera from her and carefully set it down on a nearby table.

Placing his hands at her waist and pulling her against him, he said, "I think you have enough pictures of me looking like a fool. So quit teasing me, and let me kiss you."

Wrapping her arms around his neck as goose bumps raced over her body, Valynn looked up into his alluring blue eyes and said, "Okay."

Jensen's skin was smooth and warm; wherever Valynn's body was flush with his, she could feel heat emanating from him. His head descended to hers without pause, and she felt her knees buckle a little as his mouth seized hers.

Jensen's kiss was something akin to fierce—demanding fervid reciprocation—and it caused Valynn to begin trembling inside. All of his kisses each time he'd kissed her before had transported her soul to some sort of euphoria she'd never known before. But this kiss was even more affecting, interlaced with a dominating physical element that made Valynn feel out of control—vulnerable yet extraordinarily ambitious.

"Golly!" Valynn exclaimed in a whisper when Jensen paused their kissing a moment. "If I'd known you liked the vintage '40s look on a girl, I would've been dressing like this for work from day one."

Jensen grinned. "I like you…no matter what you're wearing," he mumbled. His smile broadened as he teased, "And I'd like you even if you weren't wearing anything."

"Well, well, well! And what do we have here?"

Valynn gasped, gently pushing herself out of Jensen's arms and stepping back from him at the sound of Paula's voice.

"Hey there, Paula," Jensen greeted.

Valynn was blushing to the tips of her toes, but Jensen appeared to be completely unaffected by Paula's sudden appearance.

"Valynn and me were just doing a photo shoot project for gallery night," he said, retrieving his shirt from the floor. "With a little necking in between to motivate me."

"Necking?" Valynn gasped in a whisper.

"Oh, well, that's nice," Paula said. "I just left some proofs on my desk that I needed for my stuff, and I saw the lights on in here and figured I better check it out." Paula winked at Valynn, adding, "And I'm glad I did. It's always nice to get little preview of what everyone else's projects are for gallery night."

"Well, I hope you enjoyed it," Jensen chuckled as he slipped his shirt back on.

"Oh, believe me, I did," Paula giggled. She looked at Valynn and said, "You look awesome, Valynn!"

"Thanks," Valynn managed.

Paula winked at her again. "And that shade of lipstick looks great on you both."

"Be gone, pest," Jensen said, nodding to Paula as if he were dismissing a servant and added, "and remember, everyone's work for gallery night is supposed to be a surprise. So no telling anyone what we were working on. Got it?"

Paula laughed, making a gesture as if she were locking her lips with a tiny key. "Mum's the word, Magic Mike."

"Out," Jensen laughed, pointing to the room's exit.

"I'm going, I'm going," Paula said as she turned to leave. Pausing for a moment, however, she glanced over her shoulder and said, "Good job, Valynn! We've been trying to loosen the Reverend Wolfe up for years!"

"Good-bye, Paula," Jensen chuckled.

"Bye-bye now. And you two have fun working on your…um, your gallery night projects," Paula said as she left the room.

Once Paula was gone, Valynn recognized that the romantic moments she'd been spending with Jensen had been spoiled. But she wasn't ready to give him up yet.

So picking up her camera with one hand and taking Jensen's hand with her other, she began pulling him toward the studio exit.

"Come on! Let's download my shots of you and see what I have to work with," she giggled.

"Oh, hell no!" Jensen exclaimed emphatically, however. He tugged at her hand where it held his and said, "It's bad enough I let you talk me into shooting me. But you really don't think I can tolerate looking at myself, do you?"

Valynn shook her head as she studied the expression of earnest embarrassment on his handsome face.

"You really don't believe that you're the cutest boy ever, do you?" she asked.

Jensen frowned. "Of course not," he confirmed. "I have a mirror, into which I gaze at this caveman chin every morning."

Valynn exhaled a sigh of exasperation. "All right then. I'll just download my shots, and you'll have to wait until gallery night to see yourself in the same light the rest of the world sees you."

Jensen grinned. "Fine." He dropped her hand and retrieved his own camera. "Bring it on, baby, because I've got my own project to work on."

"Fine," Valynn giggled.

"Oh, but one more thing before you head off to horrify yourself with those images," Jensen said.

"What's that?" Valynn asked, ignoring his self-deprecating comment.

"Just sit down for a moment, okay?" he instructed, pulling a chair over for her to sit in.

"All right," Valynn agreed. Sitting down in the chair, she asked, "Now what?"

"Cross your legs…all feminine like fancy ladies do," he instructed.

Valynn crossed her legs as she watched Jensen adjust the settings on his camera.

"Now what?" she asked as he unexpectedly hunkered down in front of her.

"I just have to know one thing," he said.

"Okay…" she prodded.

Without warning then, Jensen set his camera on the floor next to Valynn's feet and took her left leg that was crossed over her right in his hands.

Goose bumps the size of cantaloupes broke out over Valynn's arms and legs then as Jensen actually ran his face over the surface of her shin. Griping the arms of the chair, Valynn gasped and literally felt dizzy with euphoria as Jensen pressed a lingering kiss to her knee.

Releasing her leg and retrieving his camera from the floor, Jensen stood up, grinned at her, and said, "I just wanted to see if those silk stockings feel as sexy as they look."

"You did?" Valynn breathed.

"Yep," he answered. He winked at her, lowered his voice, and said, "And they do." Striding away from her, leaving her weak-kneed and trembling in the chair, he said, "Good luck on your gallery night project. If you're really planning to use anything you shot today, you're sure gonna need it."

Just as Jensen had known they would be, his shots of Valynn in her vintage attire were incredible! As he drove home later that afternoon, he thought that any photographer using any kind of camera could've snapped the shutter at Valynn, all dolled up like some brunette Ginger Rogers, and come out with a fabulous result.

Still, he knew that his skills were better than the average Joe's, and so was his equipment, and it sure showed in the images he'd captured of her. After downloading his shots, Jensen had quickly settled on which image to use for one of his pieces for his gallery night gala. It was a timeless, beautiful image of Valynn—a throwback-type shot that captured the essence of the glamorous old black-and-whites of movie stars of the 1940s. Most importantly, he knew Valynn would love his work—love seeing herself presented in all the sparkling resplendence of an era where women had been wholly feminine and bewitchingly beautiful.

Valynn herself was so feminine—so beautiful—and she had no idea that she had her boss completely wrapped around her little finger. Jensen smiled as he thought that she might as well strap a bridle on him and pair of reins—because that's how much control she had over him. She didn't know it yet, thank goodness, but she did.

As he pulled into his driveway, Jensen thought about all the compliments Valynn had given him. It warmed him inside to know that she had figured out he wasn't comfortable with his appearance—that she endeavored to encourage him toward having more confidence in himself in that regard. Furthermore, she hadn't once mentioned how hot some other guy was—hadn't spent even one second going on and on about how rock solid some other man's abs were. She even seemed sincere when telling him she liked his chin. And that was *huge* to Jensen—even though he knew it shouldn't be.

As he walked into his house and tossed his keys and wallet on top of the fridge, his thoughts moved to more serious venues where Valynn was concerned. She seemed to be a throwback of sorts, a girl who valued the things of the past—things like preparing a traditional fried-chicken picnic—a girl who actually owned a red-and-white–checkered picnic blanket. And he knew she loved history and old photographs—loved them even more than she hated lemonade and feces. But he wondered how she felt about other traditions—traditions like marriage and family.

Taking a package of deli roast beef out of the refrigerator, Jensen collapsed on his sofa and turned on the TV. He had to get his mind off Valynn. He'd only known her a bit over a month, after all. It didn't seem right to be so obsessed with her—at least not yet.

Yet, as an old black-and-white film noir popped up on the television, with the female lead dressed in a black dress with shoulder pads and victory rolls pinned all over her head, Jensen sighed with giving in. It looked like he was going to have a hard time getting his mind off Valynn that night. Maybe even for the rest of his life.

♥

"*Ay caramba*!" Valynn breathed as she lay in bed, staring into Jensen's fascinating blue eyes. "You are too beautiful for words, dreamboat boy," she said aloud, running her fingertips over the 8-by-10 photograph she'd printed off before leaving the office that night.

Feeling like some lovesick school girl with a crush on the latest boy band lead singer, Valynn giggled as she kissed the incredible image of Jensen. Tucking it under her pillow—more because she was too tired to get up and put it away than because she felt like a goofy tweener—Valynn closed her eyes and smiled. She knew her gallery piece of Jensen would spin the head right off every woman scheduled to attend. And she knew it was his face that would do it, not his incredible physique. It's why she'd made the decision to use the shot she settled on—because it was a simply hypnotic image that pretty much showcased everything a real man should embody, at least to Valynn.

Humming to herself and not even realizing she was doing so, Valynn let her mind drift to the moment that day when Jensen had felt her seamed silk stockings with his cheek and then kissed her knee. The mere memory caused goose bumps to erupt over her arms and legs again, and Valynn quivered with the returned feeling of bliss that escorted her to sleep.

CHAPTER ELEVEN

"So I'm standing here looking at it with my very own eyes, and I still can't believe it," Desirae whispered aside to Valynn.

Valynn smiled as she studied the custom matted and framed photograph of Jensen. Framing had enhanced the already gorgeous image of Jensen. Valynn had decided to print the image in overall sepia, save his beautiful eyes, which were the only color in the image—blue.

"Desirae," Valynn began, "it's so perfect! You did a magnificent job."

Desirae laughed. "*You* did a magnificent job! How did you talk Jensen into this?" she said, shaking her head in residual disbelief.

"Well, as you know, it came at a heavy price," Valynn reminded her friend. She nodded toward the wall opposite of her own gallery night pieces, to where Jensen's vintage-style glamour portrait of her hung.

"Yeah, but still," Desirae said. "Getting Jensen to let you photograph him at *all*, let alone like that…" she said, nodding toward the print of Jensen again. "Girl, you worked miracles."

"Oh, I didn't do much," Valynn sighed. "The perfect subject matter pretty much presented itself."

"That's true," Desirae agreed.

Valynn smiled as she studied the large print of Jensen. She blushed a little, for she and Jensen were the only two people in the world who knew that Jensen had been looking directly at Valynn—walking toward her with the intention of kissing her—the very moment Valynn snapped the shutter and captured her handsome boss (slash boyfriend) at the perfect angle in the perfect lighting in order to produce such a perfect image.

"You were right, by the way," Desirae added in a lowered voice. "The women here tonight? Their heads about snap right off their necks when they see this sucker."

Valynn giggled, "I know, right?"

"Excuse me," an older man interrupted, tapping Desirae on one shoulder.

"Yes?" Desirae asked in turning to face him.

"Are you the woman who does all the framing for Jensen?" the well-dressed man asked.

"Yes, I am," Desirae confirmed.

"Well, I've just bought a print of this pretty pin-up girl back over here, and I was wondering if I might have you frame it just the way you have the original," the man explained. "It seems the original has already been spoken for this evening, but Jensen said you can do the same sort of matting and framing for me."

"Of course," Desirae assured the man. "Come with me, and I'll take the order myself, all right?"

"Thank you," the man said.

"Nice job, Miss Wickley, the vintage pin-up girl," Desirae whispered to Valynn as she left with the man.

Valynn blushed at the thought of her portrait—her original Jensen Wolfe portrait—hanging in some ghastly law office or something. Still, it was extremely flattering to know that Jensen's skills had made her own image so popular at the event. And he was the most incredible photographer, after all. Valynn knew that Jensen could make any woman look glamorous. But she was still flattered by the popularity of her portrait with the gallery night attendees.

As Valynn moseyed over to study Paula's pieces once more, she smiled to herself. The past few weeks had been nothing short of wondrous! The trip to Netherlander Park to recon the place for Mike and Jennifer's engagement photo shoot had been the beginning. The beefcake and glamour photo shoots that following Saturday had then acted as the catalyst to Valynn and Jensen's becoming a couple.

In truth, she couldn't believe how fast it had all happened—and sometimes wondered if it really had happened. Valynn had been especially insecure when Jensen had had to travel for two weeks on a trip to New York to visit his family and shoot several magazine layouts that he'd been hired to do.

But the moment he'd stepped into the office the morning of his return flight, Valynn was reassured that his feelings for her hadn't diminished one bit. Of course, it hadn't taken long for everyone at Wolfe Photography to catch on to the fact that their boss and their fellow employee were now an item. And the best part was that everyone was sincerely elated about it.

"Oh, look at this, Burton!" Valynn heard a woman behind her exclaim. The voice was coming from the general direction of Valynn's work, so she turned around to see if the excitement was over something she'd done.

"That's incredible," a tall older man said as he strode to stand beside a well-dressed woman looking to be about his own age. "And these are restored photographs then?"

Jensen was with the couple, and he answered, "Yes." He gestured toward the place where the bent-up bride photograph was displayed on the wall next to the restored and framed version. "You see how the bends and breaks in the image—even the dirt, silvering, and foxing—have been removed or repaired?" he asked, pointing from one image to the other. "It's incredible, isn't it?"

"Oh my, yes!" the woman next to Jensen agreed. "Just beautiful!"

"Can this be done with any old family photographs?" the man named Burton inquired.

"Ninety-nine percent of them, yes," Jensen affirmed. "The photographer that does our restorations is extremely skilled, both at restoration and original photography."

Valynn smiled, delighted by the way Jensen always felt the need to leave a one percent chance open on anything—just for the sake of Murphy's Law.

"Well, we'd be very interested in having some restoration done. We certainly would, wouldn't we, Cara?" Burton said.

"Yes," the woman named Cara agreed.

Valynn suppressed a giggle as she saw that the woman's attention had moved to Valynn's tasteful, but still beefcakey, print of Jensen. "Is this by the same person who does the restoration work?" Cara asked.

Valynn noted the way Jensen's face turned a little red. "Uh...yes," he stammered. "And this is her work as well," he added, redirecting the woman's attention to a colorful autumn landscape Valynn had prepared for the event.

"Oh, that *is* marvelous!" Cara gasped with admiration.

"Truly," Burton concurred.

Valynn did laugh a little, however, when the Cara's neck craned as she looked back to Jensen's portrait and said, "Marvelous indeed."

"You two were meant for each other, you know?" Paula whispered to Valynn as she stepped up to stand beside her.

"Oh, I hope so," Valynn admitted with a sigh.

"Oh, you are. Don't worry," Paula reassured her. "I mean, let's forget everything else about you two...and what's going on romantically between you," Paula began. "Your work is outselling everyone else's so far tonight...except for Jensen's, that is. He's making a killing, of course."

"Well, that's very kind of you, Paula, to try and encourage the novice like that," Valynn said, smiling at her friend.

"But I'm serious," Paula assured her. "I keep very careful tabs on what everyone's selling at these gallery nights. And so far, it looks like Jensen will be handing you at least three thousand dollars Monday at our luncheon. And there's still an hour to go tonight."

Valynn's brows puckered in not understanding. "What do you mean? Why would he be handing me three thousand dollars at lunch on Monday?"

Paula looked at Valynn in disbelief. "Are you kidding?" she asked. "Didn't anyone tell you?"

"Tell me what?" Valynn asked.

"That Jensen gives everyone their individual net earnings from tonight," Paula explained.

"What?" Valynn exclaimed in astonishment.

"Yeah," Paula continued. "I tally up everything everyone sold, deduct sales tax and printing and framing costs, and then when we have our office lunch on Monday, Jensen hands everyone an envelope full of cash—you know, the net of what your individual pieces brought in tonight. You're up to almost three grand so far."

Valynn looked back to where Jensen stood with another guest—a guest who seemed to be closely examining one of Desirae's pieces.

"That's...that's, like, so philanthropic," Valynn mumbled.

"Yeah. I've always thought so too," Paula agreed. "But you know Jensen. He feels like we should all enjoy the rewards of our personal work, you know?" Paula took a sip from the glass in her hand and then added, "And besides, by my calculations, Jensen's up to about one hundred grand already on his stuff. So he's doing all right for himself." She lowered her voice, adding, "You know that timed exposure he did—'Diamonds in the Desert'—the city of Albuquerque at night?"

"Yeah?" Valynn whispered.

"Some company paid Jensen fifteen thousand for some kind of limited copyrights to just that one image. So you can see why Jensen makes so much," Paula explained.

"Wow!" Valynn breathed.

Valynn smiled as Jensen glanced over at her and winked.

"Yep, you two were meant for each other, Valynn," Paula said. "A real-life happily ever after sort of thing, you know?"

"Excuse me, ma'am?" someone said from behind Paula. "I'd like to order a limited edition print of one of Mr. Wolfe's images."

"Of course," Paula said, smiling at the customer. "See you later," she whispered to Valynn before turning to leave.

As for Valynn, she simply continued to stare at the dreamboat who was the every desire of her heart. Jensen was so handsome, so talented, and such a good kisser.

"You just sold another one of those Jensen beefcake prints, Valynn," John chuckled quietly as he strode past her. "Good job on that one, girl."

"Tell that to Jensen's parents and their attractive gene pool," she whispered quickly in response.

Jensen smiled as Valynn returned his wink. He couldn't wait for the event to be over so he could hold her and kiss her a bit before dropping her home after a very long day and a very, very long night.

"Damn, I love that girl," he breathed.

"What's that, Jensen?" Nick Phillips asked.

"Oh, nothing," Jensen said, returning his attention to his guest. "Just talking to myself."

"Well, I gotta tell you, Jensen," Nick began, "you won the lottery when you snatched up this Valynn Wickley woman."

"Yeah?" Jensen asked, proudly. "You like her restorations?"

"Yes, they're flawless!" Nick exclaimed. "And her original works are awesome, as well. In fact, I'd watch your back. She's liable to get poached."

"What?" Jensen asked, suddenly snapping to full attention. "Have you heard something?"

Nick glanced around and lowered his voice, answering, "Baxter's people were in here earlier…as you know. You know how they have to keep an eye on everyone else in the business."

"Yeah…so?" Jensen prodded.

"Well, I heard one of them on the phone with Baxter himself…asking how much he'd be willing to pay the best photo restorer in the state," Nick said. "And one of the freelancers from Scenic West was here and told me that Valynn Wickley's work looked like a perfect fit for Scenic West and asked me if I knew how much it would take to pull her away from Wolfe Photography."

Jensen felt sick to his stomach. It wasn't that he was worried about losing Valynn as an employee—as an irreplaceable part of his company. He was worried about losing Valynn herself!

"Do you think she's firm with Wolfe?" Nick asked.

"I do," Jensen answered. "But I…I wouldn't want to hold her back from something like Scenic West. Baxter's an idiot—treats his people like dirt and doesn't appreciate their talent. Valynn wouldn't go there. She wouldn't want to. But if something profound comes along to send her photography career into overdrive…I-I wouldn't want to hold her back, you know?"

Jensen felt Nick's hand on his shoulder. "You feeling okay, man? You look a little peaked all of a sudden."

"I'm good, Nick," Jensen said, forcing a smile of reassuring his guest. "I just don't like hearing that someone's thinking of poaching from me, you know?"

"I do," Nick said. "But I thought you'd want to know."

"I definitely appreciate it, man," Jensen said. Forcing himself into host mode once more, he asked, "Did you see anything you liked tonight?"

"Yeah," Nick affirmed. "I ordered a print of Paula's Americana piece—the kids running through the sprinklers? That will be great in my downtown office. It helps the kids I treat feel more, you know, hopeful and happy."

"Yeah, I thought of you when she unveiled it this morning," Jensen said. "By the way, do you still want me to meet you at the hospital on the fifteenth for terminal patient portraits?"

"Absolutely," Nick assured him.

"All right then," Jensen said. "Enjoy the rest of your evening, Nick. And thanks for the heads-up on my girl getting so much attention from competitors, okay?"

"Any time, Jensen," Nick said, shaking Jensen's hand. "You're the best in the city, man, and a good guy. It's why I admire you, as well as your work."

"Thanks," Jensen said, forcing a grateful smile.

Nick chuckled. "And after seeing that...uh, very flattering picture of you over there—the one taken by your newest acquisition to Wolfe—I don't think anyone will be poaching her anytime soon, right?"

"I hope not," Jensen said. He patted Nick on one shoulder, saying, "Enjoy the rest of the night, Nick. And thanks again."

"Anytime, Jensen."

Jensen needed some air. A whole world of anxiety had just been heaped on him. Sure, he knew Valynn was a talented photographer and photo restorationist. But he'd been too busy falling in love with her over the past couple of months to think about the fact that she might not want to settle in at Wolfe—that she might not want to settle down with him. The truth of it was that Jensen had been thinking about asking Valynn to marry him for over a month! The only thing keeping him from proposing was the fact that they'd only been dating officially for a little over five weeks, and he was afraid she'd think he was nuts if he asked her so soon.

But now—now the information Nick had just given to him caused an entirely new venue of worry to overwhelm him. What if Valynn *wanted* a huge career in photography? What if her dream of getting on with Wolfe Photography was just the tip of the iceberg where her ambitions were concerned?

After all, Jensen himself had been pretty floored at how incredible her original shots for the gallery night were. The woman was truly gifted—uniquely so—and Jensen wondered, if a gig came along for Valynn with Scenic West, would she leave Wolfe? Would she leave him? And if she asked him first what he thought she should do, should he let her go so that she could follow a bigger dream-come-true than he could ever give her at Wolfe?

The stupid age-old adage—*If you love something, let it go*—began running through Jensen's mind like a repetitive song lyric. He didn't want to let her go! He loved her more than he'd ever loved anyone in all his life. He wanted her there with him—every day—every moment! He needed her. She made him happy.

But in his gut—in the deepest region of his soul—Jensen knew he would do whatever made *Valynn* the happiest, no matter the cost to his own heart, his own life—which would be little more than depressing and bleak without her.

Stepping out the back door of the showroom and into the warm night air, Jensen attempted to calm himself. After all, maybe Scenic West wouldn't offer Valynn anything. And he was pretty sure she'd never have anything to do with his biggest competitor, Norm Baxter. Yet even as he began to get control of his anxieties, he thought of how selfish he was to be hoping Valynn would make it through the aftermath of gallery night without receiving any offers.

And anyway, he had to wrap up gallery night before he could move on to worrying about anything else. He rubbed his temples with one hand, remembering that he had the big photos shoot with Brian Collins on Monday. He shook his head, wondering what in the world had come over him that found him agreeing to shoot that guy. But that was Monday. First order of business was to make it through gallery night—be the gallant host to customers who might want to purchase prints that were being shown by him and everyone he worked with.

So taking a deep breath of resolve to try not to worry about losing Valynn at any given moment, Jensen raked a hand through his hair and returned to the showroom. What would happen would happen—and he'd just have to deal with the waves of disaster as they came.

♥

"But you're not really going to hand me four thousand dollars, are you?" Valynn asked as Jensen parked in front of her house.

Jensen smiled at her, and as always, butterflies began to flutter in her stomach. "Why not?" he asked. "You earned it, didn't you?"

"Well…I guess," she stammered. "Though in truth, Paula said I sold more prints of your picture than I did any others."

She loved the fact that Jensen blushed a little. "I still can't believe you talked me into that," he said. "You know I'll never hear the end of it from some of those people who were there tonight…people I've known for years and years."

Valynn sighed, however, leaned across the truck console, and kissed him softly on the mouth. "Oh, they all loved it, and you know it. But it sure sounds like you're going to have to fork out a wad of cash at lunch on Monday. It seems like everyone made a killing tonight!"

"Well, I hope I do get to fork out a wad to everybody," Jensen said. "Everyone deserves it. It's one thing to work for a company, but it's an entirely different thing to be recognized for your own work—your individual talent, you know?" He shrugged, adding, "Plus, it's just more fun to get a cash bonus this way—for your own stuff, right?"

"Yeah, it is," Valynn admitted.

She studied Jensen for a few lingering moments. He looked tired—worried even.

"Are you okay?" she ventured. "You seem…worried or something."

But Jensen smiled, reached over, and took her chin in one strong hand as he kissed her. "Just tired," he said. "Gallery night is a lot of work in a lot of ways."

"Yeah," Valynn agreed—though she didn't believe the stressed look in his eyes was due merely to fatigue.

"Oh," he said then. "I forgot. I have something for you."

Instantly Valynn's heart leapt in her chest! She felt breathless with anticipation, and she hated that she did. Every time Jensen said something similar, her heart would soar with hoping he would pull a small velvet jeweler's box out of his pocket and proceed to propose marriage to her. It was a ridiculous expectation, of course—but she couldn't help it.

Jensen reached behind his seat, however, retrieving a white cardboard photo mailer. "Here," he said, offering it to her. "I came across these the other day and knew you would fall in love with them."

Although she was disappointed that Jensen had handed her a photo mailer instead of a diamond ring and a marriage proposal, she was excited all the same. She loved photographs, after all. Furthermore, she knew that if Jensen was giving them to her, then they were most likely superb in one way or the other.

"Okay, if you're giving them to me, they have to be incredible," she said, speaking some of her thoughts aloud.

Jensen grinned and said, "I hope so."

Valynn opened the photo mailer and withdrew a small stack of antique cabinet cards. The first thing she noticed about the beautiful old images was that every one of them was in supreme condition, as if they'd only been taken yesterday. Next she noticed that there were five cards in the stack—all wedding photos!

"*Ay caramba*, Jensen!" she exclaimed as she carefully leafed through the photos. "These are in excellent condition! And look how beautiful each couple is. This couple here is even smiling! Where did you find these?"

"Oh, if I tell you that, you'll want to come over and live with me so you can have accesses to the huge lot of photographs I purchased last week when an old photography studio was found in an abandoned building in Colorado. There were boxes and boxes of proofs and pictures that some guy had taken beginning in the 1880s, up through 1926 or so. I bought the whole lot."

Valynn squealed with delight, and Jensen chuckled, adding, "And yes, you can go through everything as soon as you have time. But meanwhile, I came across these and thought you'd like them. Not only because they're beautiful but also because…well, read what's written on the backs."

Valynn's heart began to beat with excitement as she looked at the first cabinet card photograph in the pile. A very handsome, somewhat middle-aged groom was standing next to a very beautiful, dark-haired bride. Turning the cabinet card over, she read in a whisper, "*Lawson Ipswich and Kizzy McClendon Ipswich.* And there's a wedding date…"

"Yeah, so look at the next one," Jensen urged.

Looking at the next photograph, also featuring an uncommonly handsome groom and beautiful bride, she read, "*Brake McClendon and Amoretta Ipswich McClendon.*"

"Wait for it. Wait for it…" Jensen teased.

The next cabinet card in the pile was of a lovely young blonde bride and again a uniquely handsome groom. "*Rowdy Gates and Calliope Ipswich Gates*," Valynn breathed. "Wow!"

Wedding portraits of two more exceptionally attractive couples—*Hutchner LaMontagne and Evangeline Ipswich LaMontagne* and *Warren Ackerman and Shay Ipswich Ackerman*—completed the set of cabinet cards, and it was obvious they were indeed a set—a set of wedding cabinet cards from a single family.

"They're phenomenal, Jensen!" Valynn exclaimed. Tears welled to her eyes as she thought of what a perfect gift the man she loved had given her. She even silently scolded herself for being so selfish at first—to think she'd been disappointed when Jensen had produced photographs instead of an engagement ring.

"Do you like them?" Jensen asked.

Valynn looked at him with the moisture of emotion brimming in her eyes. "I love them, and you know it," she said. Carefully putting the pictures back into the photo mailer, Valynn threw her arms around Jensen's neck, kissing him squarely on the mouth. "But are you sure you want to give them up? They're in such rare and wonderful condition…and so perfectly beautiful. Two of the couples are even smiling! You could probably sell them for a mint."

Jensen sighed as he gazed into her eyes. "Nobody would love them the way you will. And besides, I figured maybe I'd rack up a few brownie points with these."

"A few?" Valynn giggled. "How about a million?"

She kissed him again and melted to him—as much as she could melt to him over the truck's console—as he took her face between his strong hands and made love to her mouth with his passionate kiss.

"I love you, you know," Jensen mumbled against her lips.

Valynn grinned. "But not nearly as much as I love you," she whispered.

"Well, I suppose we'll see about that, won't we?" Jensen teased.

Valynn kissed him again and again to prove to him that she loved him more—more than anything—ever.

CHAPTER TWELVE

"Well, Scenic West is on the phone with Valynn as we speak," Paula said, dismally collapsing into the chair in front of Jensen's desk. "That's the fifth phone call she's gotten from either a competitor or magazine today. The vultures sure didn't waste any time, did they?"

When Jensen didn't respond, Paula ventured, "She won't leave, Jensen. You know that, don't you?"

"No. I don't," Jensen growled, looking up from his computer screen. "Valynn's got more talent in her little finger than most people do in their whole body. And like it or not, she deserves more than she'll get here."

Paula shook her head. "Now that's just nonsense, Jensen," she scolded. "You're letting doubt cloud your thinking. I mean, I know Valynn is talented, but all of us know her ambitions where her career stand end right here at Wolfe. Her ambitions where her life stand, however, end with you."

But Jensen shook his head. "I don't have time to worry about how many phone calls Valynn is getting from poachers today, Paula," he grinched. "I've got the son of…that jerk Brian Collins coming in in about an hour, and I have a feeling I'm going to regret agreeing to shoot him. So let's just focus on getting through that before I go over to Baxter's and cut his throat for trying to poach my…my…my photo restoration person."

"Okay, boss," Paula said, rising from her chair to take her leave.

It was far beyond mildly obvious that Jensen was in a foul mood. Furthermore, it was far more than mildly obvious that he was worried Valynn would choose a career with some other photo agency or magazine over Jensen. And although Paula knew Valynn wanted to stay with Wolfe and with Jensen, she also knew that Jensen would have to find out for himself.

"I'll let you know when Brian Collins and his people arrive," she said.

"Thanks, Paula," Jensen mumbled. "And please remind John to recheck the lighting in the big studio. I want everything ready so I don't have to spend any more time with that jerk than I have to, okay?"

"You bet, boss," Paula said.

"And don't call me boss, please," Jensen added. "You only call me that when you're irritated with me…and I don't like it."

"Okay, you idiot," Paula corrected herself, fairly sprinting from Jensen's office then.

Once she was back to her own office, Paula sat down in her chair, exhaling a heavy sigh. Gallery night had been very successful—financially, that was. As far as what it had done to Jensen—well, that was a disaster.

Nick Phillips had confided in Paula what he'd told Jensen about Baxter's spies and Scenic West's freelancer. Thus, she wasn't at all surprised to find Jensen in a foul mood when she'd arrived at work that morning. She knew what he was afraid of—that he wasn't worth more to Valynn than some glamorous career. But Paula knew the truth. And even though she could've wrung Jensen's neck for doubting the depth of Valynn's feelings for him, Paula knew it would all work itself out in the end. She knew it would, or at least she hoped it would.

But she could do nothing but simply wait and see what happened. She'd let Jensen get past the Brian Collins shoot, and then she'd watch events unfold. Moreover, if Paula sensed a bump in the road somewhere, she'd drop some hints to Valynn herself. Either way, Paula was confident that all would be well. Jensen and Valynn were too wonderful together, too perfectly made for each other, and far too deeply in love for anything to pull them apart. She knew it.

♥

"This guy's a piece of work!" John whispered to Valynn as they stood in the back of the studio watching Jensen's shoot of Brian Collins.

"Tell me about it," Valynn whispered in response. "He full on grabbed my butt when I was showing him where the restrooms were. Full on! Then he said he'd like to take me in the bathroom with him, throw me down on the floor, and...well, nevermind. But he's a total bottom feeder."

"Does Jensen know he said that to you? That he touched you?" John asked.

Valynn looked up to see John frowning at her with concern. "No," she answered. "Of course not! Jensen was already so stressed out about this shoot—you know, wishing he'd never agreed to do it—that I figured he didn't need any more stress." She nodded toward the setup where Brian Collins was arguing with Jensen about positioning. "I figure, let's just get this over with and toss the guy out, you know? Then Jensen can relax and get back to normal. He's been uptight about this all weekend."

But John was still frowning at her. "You should've told Jensen what the guy did…what he said."

Valynn shrugged. "All it would've done was upset him, and I don't want to add to his…"

But John wasn't listening anymore. In fact, he was striding directly toward Jensen.

"Hey, John," Valynn called. "Hey, don't…don't…"

But it was too late. Valynn watched as John tapped Jensen on one shoulder and began telling him something in a lowered voice.

"What's going on, man?" the idiot Brian Collins began ranting. "You're wasting my time! You're lucky my man hired you for this job, Jensen Wolfe! And I can fire you so fast it will make your head spin."

But Jensen wasn't listening to Brian Collins. Instead, he was frowning—frowning at Valynn.

Valynn gasped as Jensen set his camera down and started striding toward her like a lion intent on devouring his prey.

"Did this trench coat touch you, Valynn?" Jensen growled. "Did he say he wanted to—"

"Yes…yes, he did," Valynn interrupted. She could see that Jensen was infuriated, and she wanted to calm him down as quickly as possible. "But it wasn't anything I couldn't handle, Jensen. You know guys like this. They're total…"

Jensen didn't wait for her to finish, however. Storming back to where he'd left his camera, he hunkered down, ejecting the memory card and stomping on it with the heel of his boot to smash it.

"Get out!" he shouted to Collins. "You get out of my studio…now!"

"What? Who are you to be telling me what to do, little man?" argued Brian Collins, who Valynn judged couldn't have weighed more than one hundred fifty pounds and was at least six inches shorter than Jensen.

But Jensen was not a man to disrespect or mess with, and Valynn watched as he reached out, taking hold of the manager's shirt collar. "Your rock star laid his filthy hands on my girlfriend, man. He spoke to her, as well, and that I do not allow. So get his ratty a…get him out of here now."

"But we're paying you fifteen grand," the manager stammered.

"I won't shoot this idiot for all the money in the world," Jensen growled. "Now get him out."

By now, Valynn was worried—frightened even. Jensen was so angry, and he was throwing a lot of money away as well.

Paula had been standing in the back of the room with several others. Walking over to stand next to Valynn, she asked, "What happened?"

"John told Jensen that Collins…well, he grabbed my butt and said something gross to me earlier and—" Valynn began to explain.

"Oh well, that explains it then," Paula said. "I hope Jensen lays him out."

"But, Paula!" Valynn exclaimed. "It's fifteen thousand dollars!"

"It's you," Paula said, forcing a smile as she looked at Valynn. "And he's already scared you're going to leave—you know, with all these calls you're getting this morning."

Valynn was horrified! "But I would never leave Wolfe!" she assured her friend.

"Oh, Jensen's not worried about you leaving his company, Valynn. He's worried you'll leave him," Paula said.

"Get him out of my building!" Jensen shouted, drawing Valynn's attention back to Jensen's argument with Brian Collins and his manager. "You get him out of here in the next ten seconds, or I'll beat him to a pulp and drink his blood from a boot! Do you get me?"

Valynn gasped, covering her mouth with her hand in astonishment—even as everyone else in the room from Wolfe Photography began to applaud.

"All right, all right," the manager said. "Come on, Brian. There are other photography firms in the city—firms smart enough to treat their clients the way they deserve to be treated."

"You don't think I'm treating this guy the way he deserves to be treated, hmm?" Jensen growled.

"It's okay, Jensen," John said, stepping between Jensen and the manager as Jensen pushed up his shirtsleeves as if readying for a fight.

"Whatever, man," Brian Collins said, stepping away from the backdrop and lighting and heading for the door. "The dude's just some wanna-be that managed to get his hands on a nice piece of—"

But as Jensen lunged toward Brian Collins, both the narcissistic celebrity and his weasel of a manager high-tailed it double-time out through the studio exit.

Instantly, Jensen turned and started for Valynn again. As he reached her, he took her shoulders between his powerful hands and, still shaking with residual anger, asked, "Why didn't you tell me what happened, Valynn?"

Tears of guilt in causing Jensen such profound distress welled in Valynn's eyes, spilling over her cheeks as she said, "Well, it's not the first time some creep has said something gross to me…and you've been so uptight all weekend. I know something is bothering you, and I knew you were stressed about this shoot." She paused, shrugged, and said, "And it didn't seem like that big of a deal. I mean, all celebrity rock star guys have a reputation of being like that, don't they?"

"It doesn't mean you put up with it, Valynn," Jensen grumbled. He released Valynn, inhaled a deep breath in attempting to calm himself, and then said, "Can you guys all give us a few minutes please?"

"You bet," John said as he hurried from the room.

"Of course," Paula said, following suit. Everyone who had been in the room exited just about as quickly as Brian Collins and his manager had.

Once Valynn had Jensen to herself, she asked, "What's wrong, Jensen? Please, tell me! You're freaking me out! I mean, do you want to stop seeing me? Have I done something wrong?"

Jensen snapped to then. Looking at Valynn, he felt the weight of heavy guilt settle over him.

"Absolutely not," he told her, brushing the tears from her cheeks. He looked away a minute, knowing he needed to come clean. Whether or not she chose to leave him in favor of a promising career with Scenic West or any other venue that was looking to recruit her, he had to confess his fears.

"I…um…talked to a guy the other night," he began, "a friend of mine. And he told me that there was a lot of interest from other companies—interest in trying to poach you from me."

"What?" Valynn asked in a whisper. "You mean…are you talking about the phone calls I've been getting this morning? Because I would never, ever, ever leave Wolfe for any other job…ever! I thought you knew that, Jensen!"

Jensen felt his eyes narrow—felt a worried frown pucker his brow. "But what if you want to, Valynn? What if someone like Scenic

West offers you a gig that would launch your photography career to the moon? I wouldn't hold you back from that…at least I shouldn't."

"Jensen, you think I want a career in photography?" Valynn asked.

Jensen studied her expression for a moment. She seemed legitimately confused.

"Well, yeah," he admitted. "On your application…before we hired you…you said—"

"I wanted to work for you!" Valynn interrupted. "I wanted to work for the best firm in the city, so I could use my skills to make a living until…well, until what I really want to do is possible—if it's even possible anymore."

"What?" Jensen asked. "You don't want to be a professional photographer?"

"No!" Valynn assured him. "At least, not in the way you're thinking."

"But you're an incredible talent," Jensen said. "If you don't want that—if you just said that on your application because you wanted a job here—then what do you want?"

Valynn paused in answering him. She'd never told Jensen about her dreams of what she really wanted to do with her life. And she knew that if she told him now—if it wasn't what he wanted to hear in that moment—that he might storm out of the studio as quickly as everyone else had. But in her heart she knew he wouldn't—hoped he wouldn't. She loved him, and she knew his soul—knew what kind of man he was and what he needed out of life.

"I can think of nothing more beautiful in all the world…nothing I'd rather use my camera to shoot than the husband and children I hope to have one day, Jensen," she confessed. "All my life I've dreamed of photographing my own baby's toes, my husband's handsome smile." She shrugged. "Truly, I got into photo restoration simply because I love old photographs and preserving the past. I found I could make a bit of money at it—enough to keep my parents off my back about finishing college—while I ignorantly hoped I'd fall into being able to be what I really want to be—a wife, a mom, a housewife…a woman who can take great photographs of her kids sleeping in their little beds after she's sung them to sleep, you know?"

When Jensen said nothing, just continued to stare at her with a confused frown on his face, Valynn continued, "I know it's an archaic ideal from a modern standpoint—that a lot of people think housewives are uneducated, don't have a real job, and all that. But anyone with any brains at all can see how much work it is, if you do it right, you know? I mean, I believe in all that stuff about women being treated equally in the workplace and that they should be able to have any career they want to. But that's not what I want. I want to be like my grandma was—a stay-at-home mom who has fresh cookies baked when the kids get home from school, gets to cuddle on the couch with her husband in the evenings and watch some funny sitcom…you know? I want to take pictures of life, of living life, of babies in bathtubs and toddlers with cake frosting smeared all over their faces."

Again she paused, wishing Jensen would respond. But again he was silent, just standing there staring at her.

"Say something, Jensen," she begged, wiping at the tears on her cheeks. "Take me or leave me. Just say something, please."

"So you're not going to leave me to go on some photographic adventure with Scenic West? Is that what you're saying?" Jensen asked. Slowly his frown relaxed—turned into a smile.

"Yes," Valynn answered. "I have no desire to travel around taking pictures other people want me to take. The most I ever want to do is to go on a trip to Vermont in the fall and shoot pictures of covered bridges. And I only want to do that if…if you're with me."

Jensen sighed, raking a hand through his hair. "Well, I'm still glad I sent that idiot packing just now," he said. "But…but I'm sorry I thought you might…you know, leave me."

Valynn smiled at him as she fully realized just how much he loved her. She knew then that Jensen loved her almost as much as she loved him.

"Why would I ever want to leave you?" she asked him. "You're the cutest boy I've ever known."

Jensen chuckled, gathered her into his arms, and pressed a firm kiss to the top of her head.

"Hey, why don't you do me a favor?" he began.

"What's that?" Valynn asked, melting against his warm, solid body.

"Reach into my front right pocket for me," he instructed. "I've got something in there I've been carrying around for a couple of weeks now."

Valynn arched one eyebrow as she looked up into Jensen's handsome face. "Reach into your right front pocket? Really?" she giggled.

"Really," Jensen said, smiling at her.

Suspicious that he was teasing her in some way—that she might reach and find that his pocket was full of sand or Silly Putty—nevertheless, she did. The moment her fingers felt what really was in Jensen's pocket, however, Valynn began to weep.

As she pulled her hand out of his pocket to reveal the most beautiful diamond encrusted engagement ring she'd ever seen, she gasped as tears streamed down her face.

"So?" Jensen began. "You wanna tell Scenic West to go suck on a lemon and go into business with me instead?"

"Business? Like the photography business?" Valynn stammered as Jensen took the ring from her, slipping it onto her left ring finger.

"Sure," he confirmed. "Although I was thinking more along the lines of the baby-making business, the warm cookies after school business, the sleeping with me all the time business. But the photography business is good too."

Valynn brushed the tears from her cheeks—tried to breathe normally even for the excitement and the profound joy that were welling up inside her.

"I-I thought you were going to break up with me," she confessed as she studied the ring on her finger. "I-I thought—"

"Well, I thought you were going to leave me for a mere job," Jensen countered.

"You really want to marry me?" Valynn asked.

Jensen grinned with mischief as he pushed her back against the studio wall and said, "Oh, I want to do a whole lot more than that, baby. But let's start with the marrying part, okay?" He kissed her lightly on the mouth, mumbling, "So? Will you marry me, Valynn?"

"Of course! I mean, you are the cutest boy I've ever seen," she answered.

Jensen smiled as his mouth claimed Valynn's then—claimed *her*. And as they stood there in the studio, kissing as if they'd never be able to stop kissing one another, they were almost oblivious to the applause and well-wishes of all the other employees at Wolfe Photography who stood watching—and sharing in their happiness.

EPILOGUE

As Valynn lay in hammock, she listened. All around her she could hear the soothing sounds of a summer's day—birds twittering in the trees, the tender, melodious pinging of the wind chimes hanging under the back porch, and the soft whispers of the breeze as it gently rustled the leaves of the oak nearby. The sweet fragrances of summer flowers and leaves, of green grass and potting soil from the flower pots, made her smile as it added to her tranquil enjoyment of the day.

"So? What do you think?" Jensen asked.

Opening her eyes to see her handsome husband standing watch over her and enjoying a tall glass of iced lemonade, she answered, "It's wonderful! And so comfortable! Nothing like those chord hammocks, you know?"

Jensen set his lemonade on the picnic table behind him and then stretched out next to Valynn on the new canvas hammock. "I know," he agreed. "When I tried it out at the home improvement store, I knew we had to have it." He winked at Valynn, adding, "I mean, it's not as conducive to trapping you right where I want you as that old thing at Netherlander Park was. But I think I could get the job done on this one too." He leaned over Valynn, placing a moist, wanton kiss to her mouth. "If you know what I mean."

Valynn giggled. "Oh, I know what you mean, beefcake boy." She kissed him and then gazed at him lovingly for a few moments.

"What?" Jensen asked, smiling at her.

"The house, the yard, all of it—it's so perfect! More perfect than I ever dreamed, you know?" she explained. "And the most wonderful part of it all…is you. Do you know I still wake up in the middle of the night, with you lying right there with me, holding me even…and wonder for a second if it's all real? If *you're* real?"

Jensen brushed a strand of hair from her cheek as he hovered over her. "Me too," he told her. "Me too."

Jensen's kiss never failed to thrill Valynn to her very core! But as the hot, moist flavor of his mouth mingled with her own, she suddenly began to giggle.

"What's wrong?" Jensen asked, chuckling as he ceased in kissing her long enough to ask.

"You've been drinking lemonade," Valynn explained, smiling. "I can taste it…but it didn't at all remind me of my sister's messy diaper all those years ago. Maybe I'm cured."

Jensen laughed. "Well, I'm glad my kiss doesn't remind you of baby poop," he said. "That could turn out to be a real problem, you know?"

"Well, lately, I haven't felt so weirded out about feces in general," Valynn confessed. "Especially baby poo. And that's probably a really good thing…you know, considering."

"Considering what?" Jensen asked as he brushed another strand of hair from her cheek.

"Considering that by next May we'll be having a lot of baby poo around our house." As Jensen frowned with confusion, Valynn added, "And I hope I'm over this morning sickness before we take our trip to Vermont next month."

As Jensen's brows arched with sudden understanding—as a broad smile spread over his face—he asked, "You promise you're not kidding me?"

"I promise," Valynn said, placing a kiss on his chin. She saw the excess moisture of joy gathering in Jensen's eyes and added, "And if it's a boy, I hope he has your perfect chin."

Valynn wasn't able to say anything else, for Jensen's kiss claiming her lips in expressing his love for her—his excitement about their baby—silenced her for some time. And she savored it, lingered in the bliss of her husband's affection—thankful that somehow, she'd managed to win his heart—and bathed in the wonder of knowing their first baby was growing inside her.

AUTHOR'S NOTE

I *love* photographs! In fact, I've loved photographs and taking photographs my entire life. Furthermore, I do think it's an inherited trait. One of my paternal great-grandmothers loved photos and photography, and my dad loves photos and photography (and even worked as a professional photographer). So I guess you can say it's in my blood. And that inherent love for photos and taking them didn't stop with me. My daughter, Sandy, is an incredible photographer and loves photos as much as I do!

My love for photographs began when I was when I was little, little, little, and I can remember being mesmerized by family snapshots. And by the time I was eleven or so, I'd managed to get my first cameras—a Polaroid Instant that spat out instant pictures (not very good ones but photos nonetheless) and a little 120 that used film but took even worse photographs. But that was how cameras were back then; the great 35 mm ones were *entirely* unaffordable to anyone but a pro. So most people just had their little snapshot cameras—not like now when the digital cameras are so awesome and affordable. However, I still managed to torture my parents, my dog, my little sister, and my best friend Amy thoroughly enough with my Polaroid and 120 all the same. One of my greatest photo sessions (with Amy as the victim) found Amy dressed in panty hose and a leotard, posing in front of a Mexican serape in recreating the famous Farrah Fawcett poster of the 1970s. Ha ha! My little sister was a victim in another one of my "photo shoots"—featuring her four-year-old self in a cool pair of bell-bottom pants, equally cool sunglasses, and a shirt twisted into a halter top, posed on a rock wall at a rest stop somewhere between Albuquerque and Santa Fe one summer. As you can see from this example of one of my Polaroid shots, the portraits of my little sister are epic! (My sister will probably wring my neck for including her portrait here, but it's one of my favorites ever of her and always makes me giggle and think of good times together!)

Suffice it to say, by now, if you've been reading my books for very long at all, you already know how passionate I am about photographs. Therefore, I'll quit jawing and skip right to the snippets!

Snippet #1—Photo restoration is something I wish I had the skills, equipment, programs, and especially time to delve into. The fact that it's even possible amazes me, and I think it is an invaluable gift of technology. As you can see by the photos below, it's understandable why Valynn was so emotional about photo restoration. The photographs below are of my father-in-law's parents. The original (at left below) was found in some of my father-in-law's sister's things after she passed away during Hurricane Katrina. I scanned it one day when my in-laws were staying with us, and years later when my friend Sheri began to get into photo restoration, I had her restore the photograph. The photograph at right is (obviously) the restored version. What a treasure it is to all of us in the family to be able to have the photo printed in good shape, framed and hanging on our walls! All hail photo restoration!

Snippet #2—Like Jensen and Paula, all the members of our family are *Back to the Future* fans—line-quoting, laugh-out-loud while watching it, very serious fans of that awesome trilogy of movies. And for years and years now I've attempted (and usually succeeded) in cracking my kids up by pumping my fists in the air and exclaiming, "Eighty-eight miles per hour!" whenever I've achieved even a little something. Yeah, we're dorks! Ha ha!

Snippet #3—Although Desirae (the custom framer at Wolfe Photography) makes only a couple of quick cameo appearances, her character was inspired by my real-life friend Desirae—a very, very talented artist and a very talented custom framer on the side! The moment I met Desirae and saw what beautiful framing work she does—well, let's just say, I text her and make sure she's available before taking anything in to be framed now! Desirae does a superb job on any and all frameable treasures I entrust to her (antique wedding photos, antique postcards, vintage art or text of any sort, and even *Star Wars* art for our *Star Wars* bedroom). Desirae framed all my *Two Weeks with Love* movie posters, lobby posters, and 8-by-10 black-and-white photographs of Jane Powell and Ricardo Montalbán for my fun *Two Weeks with Love*–themed laundry room. Best of all, you should see the *gorgeous* painting she did for me a couple of years ago as a Christmas gift—a beautiful still life of pumpkins and a squash! It's gorgeous and hangs in my office to inspire me and uplift my soul every day! Thanks, Desirae—you're *so* the bomb!

Snippet #4—Originally, I had titled this book something different. However, the further I got into writing it, the less I "felt" that title, you know? So, about halfway through the book, I woke up one morning and knew it needed a title that was more befitting. I love the hammock scene in this story, and I wanted to incorporate it somehow in the title. But I found that it wasn't an easy task! I mean, what was I going to title it? *The Hammock Scene*? *Love in a Hammock*? *The Hammock of Love*? (Those last two sound like old hippie movies from the '60s. All I could think of were communes and psychedelic rainbows and stuff. Ha ha!) But then I thought of what a dreamboat Valynn saw Jensen to be, and that was that—*With a Dreamboat in a Hammock*! Well, I called my daughter, Sandy (to whom the book is dedicated), to see what she thought of revamped title. She happily chirped, "I love it! It sounds like a line from an old '50s song!" Being that my Sandy inspired so much of this book and that I wrote it for her, it's perfect! Not only is Sandy a photographer and lover of old photos and all beautiful photographs, but also she loves the '50s—its music, its photographs, its history, its kitchen styles! Therefore, because my sweet, inspiring daughter, Sandy, loved the title I had chosen for this book, I love the title even more! And after all, who wouldn't want to linger with a dreamboat in a hammock, right? ☺

Snippet #5—Okay, here's the thing. As a mom of two very, good-looking young men, I've observed a lot of things girls do these days when they like a boy. And I have to say some of those things don't make any sense to me at all! For instance, girls who have liked my sons tended to talk to them about how hot *other* guys were—like, even on dates. I remember when the *Twilight* movies were big at the box office, and there was that whole Team Edward and Team Jacob thing going on, remember? Well, girls would talk to my boys about how hot Taylor Lautner is, how great his abs are. And for some reason, they expected my boys to be totally down with that line of conversation. Moms of boys and married women—you guys know what I mean. A teenage boy's or young man's self-esteem is very fragile. And when they get up the nerve to ask a girl to dance or ask her to go on a date and then spend the entire time hearing about how hot other guys are, it can be discouraging and debilitating, not to mention infuriating. So here's a little advice to all women, young or old, from a romance novelist with a dead sexy husband and two very attractive sons: guys don't want to hear about how sexy you think *other* guys are. Spend your energy building up the guy sitting next to you or standing in front of you or taking you to a movie and dinner.

And that goes for married girls as well as single girls. Husbands need reassurance that they're attractive to you and still your hero no matter what their age. I mean, to me, that's just common sense, right? We as women despise, resent, and are deeply hurt if our guys go on and on to us about how beautiful another woman is, so why shouldn't we recognize that in our men? That's not to say that once in a while a couple can't agree on the fact that there are other attractive people in the world. Just be sensitive and make it a rare thing. For instance, it took about seven or eight years into our marriage before Kevin got me to admit that I thought actor Kurt Russell was cute when I was younger and before I got Kevin to admit that he thought actress Cheryl Ladd was pretty when he was younger. (You young pups will have to look them up being that I'm sure you have no idea who they are!) And now that we're middle-aged, we are able to comfortably comment on the fact that so-and-so is really pretty or that so-and-so is really handsome. But even after thirty-one years of marriage, it's not something we touch on very often, or go on and on about, and we use words like *good-looking*, *pretty*, and *handsome* when talking about others—not *hot* or *sexy*. So in the end, build your man up; don't spend your energy putting doubt and discouragement in his mind about himself. Just a little insight from an old lady with good-lookin' sons! ☺

Snippet #6—You know Valynn's rather graphic description of how houseflies eat? It's yet another wonderful story from my childhood—via my own tell-it-like-it-is, no-holds-barred, sweetheart of a mommy! My mom did not believe in beating around the bush about stuff. When my sister or I asked her a question, she answered it—straight and with very often graphic (yet valuable) scientific information. I think it was on my sixth birthday that I learned the disgusting truth about houseflies and how they eat. Mom had made me this adorable kitty cat birthday cake, beautifully frosted in pink icing. Well, the way I remember, Mom had put the cake on the table or something, in getting ready for my little birthday party, when along comes this ugly old housefly. (Now keep in mind, this was when we lived on a dairy farm in Idaho, so I'm sure it was a big, fat fly. You know the kind that hang out on cow manure and have the sort of iridescent green bodies?) So this ugly housefly lands on my beautiful pink-iced kitty cat birthday cake. Ugh! That was gross enough in itself! But as my mom shooed away the fly, she (as she often did) launched into an educational tangent about exactly *how* flies eat. Mom explained to me (in graphic detail) exactly what Valynn explained to Jensen and Paula—the way a fly vomits on its intended food so that its juices dissolve said food into a disgusting juice that they slurp up through their proboscis. I was instantly grossed out and so thankful that my mom picked off the cake frosting where the fly had landed. Flyspecks were also a part of farm life, and I already knew what those were. And though I don't really have a problem with manure per se, flies vomiting on cakes angers me! So there you go—another kindred feeling between author and book character.

Snippet #7—The scene where Valynn nearly chokes on a piece of bread is actually based on a little incident that happened to an old boss of Kevin's years and years ago. Ron was a funny guy, actually. In truth, Kevin loves the TV series *The Office* simply because Steve Carrell's character, Michael Scott, reminds Kevin so much of Ron. In fact, Ron lent quite a lot of amusement to our lives during those years. For instance, there was the time that Ron walked around for days and days humming a tune that everyone in the office knew sounded familiar but no one could place. Until the day that the fax machine went off while everyone was sitting together in the office, and they suddenly realized that Ron's favorite tune was the fax machine sound! Ha ha! But no "Ron story" stuck with our entire family the way the "asparagus" story did. Old Ron was eating a cookie one day and started to choke. Everyone noticed and asked if he was okay. All he kept saying was, "Get me some water! My asparagus! My asparagus! There's a piece of my cookie stuck in my asparagus!" Although someone did get a glass of water for Ron and Ron was fine, the incident did amuse everyone nearly to tears—including me when Kevin related the story that evening. Therefore, from that day forward, Kevin and I have always referred to our esophagus as "My asparagus! My asparagus!"

Snippet #8—Why yes, Jensen Wolfe's first name was indeed inspired by actor Jensen Ackles! My youngest son, Trent, and I are die-hard *Supernatural* fans, and while we were rewatching Season 1 and I was reading the credits that precede the episode, I thought, "Hmm. Jensen…that's a cool first name." And so Jensen Wolfe became Jensen Wolfe! As for Valynn—I had another name in place for her, but a friend pointed out to me that, years ago, in one of my earliest books, the name I had chosen for the heroine in this book had been the name of the hero's horse in that long-ago book. Well, that just wouldn't do! I couldn't have you thinking about a hero's horse when you were reading about the heroine in here, could I? Nonetheless, I had a heck of a time finding another name I liked. Until I stumbled across "Valynn" in a purchase notification e-mail to the next day. They handed me several photographs: one was of the young woman herself, as a bride, standing in a loving pose with her handsome groom. It was a gorgeous photograph, and I told the young woman so. She thanked me and smiled. The next photograph was of the young man who was the groom in the wedding picture. He was dark-haired guy, wearing a baseball cap and a T-shirt and looking rugged and very handsome. The third was a beautiful photo of the guy and the girl standing at the altar. I asked the young woman what size she wanted the prints of the photographs to be. She discussed it with her mom, and they decided to have each photo enlarged to an 8-by-10, and they needed them within the hour. Usually our policy was to have twenty-four hours for prints. The older lady explained to me that they needed the photos that evening—for a funeral! For a funeral for the handsome guy, the young woman's husband! Apparently he'd gone missing four or five days before, and the police had found his car off the road several days later, and he was dead. At that point, I just began weeping! Here was this beautiful young woman standing in front of me, handing me her wedding picture and other pictures of her young, handsome husband—and he was gone! When I started crying, both the ladies started crying too, and we stood there for fifteen or twenty minutes while they told me what a great young man the guy had been, how heartbroken everyone was that he had died so tragically and so soon. It was heart-wrenching! I comforted them as much as I was able, promised I'd do their prints right away so they could have them in an hour, and never worked the counter again for the rest of my shift—because I couldn't quit weeping. So, even though that over the years I've learned that I have to have better control of my emotions in public and have managed to do a pretty good job of that, that particular memory always makes me cry. It's why I commiserate so just casual friends with. To me, dubbing someone with a kind nickname of endearment is a token of affection. It's an offered hand of a more intimate friendship and can often span decades, a lifetime, or even beyond. As you may already know, from the day of my birth until I was just past the age of nineteen, everyone I knew called me Skeeter instead of Marcia. The only place I was referred to Marcia was at school, by teachers and most friends there. But at home and with relatives, close friends, and anyone I met outside of school, Skeeter (sometimes Skeet) was my name. I'm guessing some people didn't even know my real name at times. It was a term of endearment given to me by my father that stuck—completely stuck until after I was married, when circumstances (long story) made the decision for me that I would start going by my given name. Even now, however, my parents, my sister, my aunt and uncles, a couple of cousins, and a few people I see once in a while still call me Skeeter. My mom, Patsy, was always called Punky, by her parents, her siblings, and my dad. Even my little grandson calls my mom Punky or Grandma Punky. And I think that was another reason I fell in love with nicknames. Unfortunately, it didn't take long before I learned that not all nicknames are kind. In fact, unkind nicknames don't even deserve to be called nicknames, you know? I loathe unkindness and cruelty, in any form, and giving people mean nicknames or rhyming yucky words with their names just ticks me off! There were a couple of rhyming-type nicknames given to me on the playground that I didn't mind too much. These would be Marcia Tortilla and Marcia Garcia. Didn't mind those at all; they even bordered on endearing. But it was second grade and Marcia Diarrhea that bugged me! Ha ha! Seriously, though it didn't stick at all past a couple of months, I still think of it when people ask me how to pronounce my name. (Of course, I should be thankful: Kevin had a great aunt everyone called Aunt

Toad for her whole entire life. It wasn't until long after she had passed away that my mother-in-law told me she had discovered her real first name was Harriet!)

Anyway, when my sister, Luanna, and I were still at home, a wonderful little family moved in across the street. The family had three children, and Luanna and I babysat them on occasion and became great friends with the entire family. Well, the oldest child was a boy, and we'll call him Joe for this story. Now, Joe had some sort of alopecia, if I remember correctly, and therefore he didn't have but a few wispy hairs on the top of his head and didn't have eyebrows or very many eyelashes. He was a kind, compassionate, helpful boy who our family adored (and still adores). One day when I was already married but still pretty young and my sister was maybe a senior in high school, Luanna and I were sitting across the table from one another, enjoying a nice conversation with Joe (maybe a middle-schooler by now). Somehow Luanna and I got on the subject of mean nicknames we'd been called as kids. I said, "Well, they used to call me Marcia Tortilla." To which Luanna replied, "They always called me Luanna Banana!" To which I replied, "Well, I got called Marcia Diarrhea!" At that point, I realized that we were leaving Joe out of the conversation a bit, so I turned to him, and in an effort to draw him into the conversation, I asked, "Did they ever call you anything in elementary school, Joe?" He hung his head a little and simply stated, "Yeah. Baldy." Is that the saddest thing ever? My sister and I felt like heels, to say the very least, and spent a good half an hour building up poor Joe's self-esteem. At that point, Luanna Banana or even Marcia Diarrhea seemed kind, compared with the mean name kids had labeled Joe with because of his alopecia. And so, there you have it: Joe my neighbor boy, my inspiration for the

Neanderthal Wolf—Jensen Wolfe, who grew up to be a dreamboat yet still had some insecurities about his physical appearance because of cruelty as a kid. Poor Jensen and poor Joe, right?

Snippet #12—In my photographer days, one of my favorite subjects was my husband Kevin. I loved to take photos of Kevin, and even though he would never let me take a true "beefcake" photo of him, he did allow me a few minutes a couple of times to shoot a few shots of him. The famous "Kevin Bookmarks" that were so popular from about 2003 to 2005 (2005 was when Kevin put the brakes on any more bookmarks) were and are some of my very favorite photos of him! My favorite of the ones he let me take in 2002 (he gave me ten whole minutes out in the mountains of Colorado on a family vacation) appears after this author's note and should be very familiar to you by now. I love the fact that my husband is so photogenic—and therefore I love that Jensen gave Valynn a chance to capture his hotness for one of her gallery pieces!

Snippet #13—And now for the most important snippet of all—a snippet about my daughter, Sandy! (Here's a photo of my Sandy wearing her hair up in a snood in the back. I love this picture of her!) For those of you who have met my Sandy, you know how beautiful she is, both inside and out! I'm so very proud of the sweet, adorable, giggling little girl she was and the beautiful, sweet, giggling, incredible woman that she has become.

Sandy is a wife and mommy above all else; those are her priorities. Growing up, she didn't dream of any career other than being a housewife and mother. Sure, she worked like a dog at any job she had—including a hair salon, landscaping, fast food, and so on. But her only true ambition was to be a modern-day June Cleaver. And just as I was when I had my children all living at home, she has been lucky enough (blessed) to be living that June Cleaver housewife dream. And yet Sandy also has tons of hobbies, the most beloved of those being photography. As you've probably already guessed, Valynn is totally based on Sandy and in so many ways is a reflection of her—and not just because of their mutual love for photography. My daughter, Sandy, has far surpassed any meager talent I may have had as a photographer! And

although she always puts her husband and babies before anything else, she is quite sought after for portraiture gigs—and paid very well when she does them! Her photos are beautiful. And one thing she loves is recreating vintage photographs. In fact, a few years ago, she grabbed a couple of wigs from somewhere and, with a little help from my (at that time soon-to-be) daughter-in-law, took some incredible selfies of herself dressed in period clothing and makeup!

Check out these two images of my 1920s flapper girl Sandy and one image of my 1930s Depression-era Sandy. Incredible, right? And these were taken before she even had her main photography equipment and high-end camera. It's why this book is dedicated to my daughter—my beautiful, talented, entirely feminine, hysterically fun, wonderful angel of a daughter. *With a Dreamboat in a Hammock* was inspired by so many aspects of Sandy's talents and personality, and it just breathes of her excitement about life, love, family, and the desire to be that stay-at-home mom who values her family more than anything in all the world. My Sandy is one of my greatest blessings, and I admire her more than she will ever understand! I love you, my Roni Pony!

Snippet #14— Like Valynn, I'm not a fan of lemonade. I'll just say this—I hate lemonade for the very same reason Valynn does! Her story is based entirely on my own experience—during a picnic up in the mountains of the Sandia Crest—as an almost eight-year-old girl with my parents and baby sister, who was nearly a year old. And there you have it—my deep-seeded, psychological reasons for not liking lemonade. On some subconscious level, I associate lemonade with baby poo! Oddly enough, my sister told me just this evening, as we were discussing my traumatizing remembrance, that she absolutely *loves* lemonade! "I'm a connoisseur of lemonade!" she joyfully exclaimed. And seriously, one has to wonder if her love for lemonade stems from the same incident that spawned my dislike for it. Hmm.

As always, I just hope you found some fun in reading this story. I hope you feel better and more like you can face the day again. I also hope you'll join me in always referring to your esophagus as asparagus and that you'll still enjoy drinking lemonade out by the pool!

Yours,
Marcia Lynn McClure

To the man of my very own dreamboat…

My husband, Kevin!

ABOUT THE AUTHOR

Marcia Lynn McClure's intoxicating succession of novels, novellas, and e-books—including *A Crimson Frost, The Visions of Ransom Lake*, *Kissing Cousins* and *Untethered*—has established her as one of the most favored and engaging authors of true romance. Her unprecedented forte in weaving captivating stories of western, medieval, regency, and contemporary amour void of brusque intimacy has earned her the title "The Queen of Kissing."

Marcia, who was born in Albuquerque, New Mexico, has spent her life intrigued with people, history, love, and romance. A wife, mother, grandmother, family historian, poet, and author, Marcia Lynn McClure spins her tales of splendor for the sake of offering respite through the beauty, mirth, and delight of a worthwhile and wonderful story.

BIBLIOGRAPHY

A Bargained-For Bride
Beneath the Honeysuckle Vine
A Better Reason to Fall in Love
The Bewitching of Amoretta Ipswich
Born for Thorton's Sake
The Chimney Sweep Charm
Christmas Kisses
A Crimson Frost
Daydreams
Desert Fire
Divine Deception
Dusty Britches
The Fragrance of her Name
A Good-Lookin' Man
The Haunting of Autumn Lake
The Heavenly Surrender
The Highwayman of Tanglewood
Kiss in the Dark
Kissing Cousins
The Light of the Lovers' Moon
Love Me
The Man of Her Dreams
The McCall Trilogy
Midnight Masquerade
An Old-Fashioned Romance
One Classic Latin Lover, Please
The Pirate Ruse
The Prairie Prince

The Rogue Knight
Romance at the Christmas Tree Lot
The Romancing of Evangeline Ipswich
Romantic Vignettes
Saphyre Snow
Shackles of Honor
The Secret Bliss of Calliope Ipswich
Sudden Storms
Sweet Cherry Ray
Take a Walk With Me
The Tide of the Mermaid Tears
The Time of Aspen Falls
To Echo the Past
The Touch of Sage
The Trove of the Passion Room
Untethered
The Visions of Ransom Lake
Weathered Too Young
The Whispered Kiss
The Windswept Flame
With a Dreamboat in a Hammock